ABOUT THIS BOOK

Cass and Kitty had been married only a few weeks but soldiers have to go where they are sent. Cass' orders took him to France. He looked forward to her letters every day.

The letter he now held in his hand was like a punch below the belt. It made his blood run cold. It told him that she was having an affair with the owner of the shop where she worked. Worse still she seemed to think that he would accept it. How could she think like that? Their marriage was not a free for all. She was the only woman in his life and he expected to be the only man in hers. No one else was invited or welcome. Because he loved her he made excuses to himself for her. She must have been lonely. Loneliness does strange things to people. She had been taken advantage of. She had been caught in a weak moment when she was down. He wrote back telling her to end it. She didn't.

His one thought was to get back to Australia and 'counsel' her lover. He would teach the slimy mongrel to leave another man's wife alone.

The war ended, at last. He was the first passenger off the plane in Melbourne. He went to the shop where Kitty worked. He confronted her lover. There was a struggle. Kitty's lover was killed. Cass was charged with murder. The court would have to decide whether her lover's death was accident or design. From the moment of his arrest and throughout the trial Cass remained silent. A group of twelve strangers would decide whether he lived or was to be hanged by the neck until he was dead. Should the jury find him guilty or innocent he would always love his wife.

ABOUT THE AUTHOR

KEN MOORE is an Anglo-Irish Australian. During his early working life he was a detective, a police inspector, and a public prosecutor. He became a barrister after graduating from Middle Temple, London. He has lived and worked in nine different countries.
He is retired after serving for 20 years as a magistrate in Perth, Western Australia.

SILENCE
IN COURT

KEN MOORE

plunge
PUBLISHING

Other books by Ken Moore:

The Gentle Kidnapper
Preston Quark's Wooden Overcoats
Preston Quark's End Game

All titles are available from: kenmoorebooks.com & plungepublishing.com

First published 2019 by Plunge Publishing.
ISBN: 978-0-9954068-8-9 (paperback)
ISBN: 978-0-9954068-9-6 (ebook)

Plunge Publishing
PO Box 82,
Ringwood East,
VICTORIA, Australia.
plungepublishing.com

 NATIONAL LIBRARY OF AUSTRALIA A catalogue record for this book is available from the National Library of Australia.

DEDICATION

For Doe, my dear wife forever loyal and true.
And for the family we both love.

To Harry & Margaret
with love & tender
thoughts of the old
days. Oh, for one
of those moments of
gladness.

Ken Moore.
15/09/2019.

ACKNOWLEDGEMENT

*With warmest thanks to Pip and Dale Rye,
our daughter and her husband, who made
Silence in Court possible.*

INTRODUCTION

"I can't impress upon you, Mr Carrington, the importance of indicating that you understand what I am saying. You are charged with murder which is the most serious offence on the criminal calendar. I require to know if you understand that. Would you be so kind, Sir, as to indicate by a verbal yes that you do?"

A magistrate calling a man in the dock, Sir, and sounding as if he meant it. That was surely unusual. You might wonder why.

Cassidy Ambrose Carrington, a trim five foot ten inches tall in the old measurement (about 178 cm), stood ram-rod straight in the dock. His dark brown hair with its parting on the left side of his head and his neatly trimmed sideburns indicated that he was a man who took a pride in his appearance. He was not a beautiful man, maybe not even handsome but there was about him that something that would have made him stand out from all the other men in a crowded room. Even without his military uniform and his sergeant's stripes it would not have taken a Sherlock Holmes to deduce that he was a military man. With his wide set grey eyes not for a moment flickering he stared at the British coat of arms which hung on the wall of the court just behind the magistrate's head. Was he looking at the scroll under the shield? That scroll which read, Dieu Et Mon Droit - God and my right. Could it be, the prosecutor wondered, that, before his God, in some strange way known only to himself, he thought that what he had done was right. Only he knew what he thought.

The magistrate, Mr Clarence Fitzgerald, was a patient man. At fifty nine years of age with fifteen years on the bench he was old enough and experienced enough both on the bench and off it to know that appearing in court caused some people, even the most stalwart, great trauma. He also knew a little of this man's antecedents and for that reason was more than usually courteous. He was an old soldier himself. The black patch he wore over his left eye was testimony to his own service in that war to end all wars which had preceded the one just finished. He had lost that eye when as a young lieutenant in France he had fought so valiantly to uphold the freedom he still so passionately held dear. In the losing of his eye he had gained a medal for rescuing one of his men in an unselfish act that saved that man's life. He did not regret his loss and he never talked about it. He thought it was a small price to pay for the joy of having a husband return to his wife and two children in Australia. Anyway, he could see more with his one eye than most men could with two. He did not think his act worth a medal. What he did he would have done again and gladly for no recognition. In his opinion it was what any comrade in arms would do for one of his mates and he, being the officer in charge, could do no less.

Mr Fitzgerald knew that war and stress do strange things to men and he wondered what part the war had to play in the life of the man before him. This was no ordinary man. Cassidy Carrington was famous in Victoria, Australia, not because of the alleged murder for which he now appeared in the dock in Melbourne city but because of his war service. Sergeant Carrington, as he then was, was the recipient of the Victoria Cross and two other medals for gallantry and held several campaign medals when the war ended and he returned to Australia. It may have been the sight and recognition of the medal ribbons on Cassidy Carrington's chest that caused Mr Fitzgerald to treat him with such courtesy. That is not to say that Mr Fitzgerald did not treat everyone who came before him with courtesy regardless of their rank or station in life. But I'd better start at the beginning.

~ THE BEGINNING ~

CHAPTER ONE

It was one week before I was due to receive my Bachelor of Laws Degree from Monash University, that university which was called after yet another famous military man. General Monash was said to have saved the lives of many and shortened the war by months through his strategic planning and military intuition. Australia owed him much. I felt the need to go and see my paternal grandfather. Grandpa and I were very close. Never a week went by when we didn't meet. Never once did he miss my birthday. Always he encouraged me. On those days when I was down and thought that I had bitten off more than I could chew by opting to do law when I could have taken something a little less exacting he would say, "Take it as a challenge, Ben. Anyone can take the easy way out. If you have as much faith in yourself as I have in you you will fly through that course. I haven't the least doubt you will lick the lot of them. So go to it. Give it your best shot and you will have no regrets. Look for the person you think is the best in your group and set out to beat them. You may not but at least you won't be bottom of the heap."

And here I was, several years later with the end in sight. I did not finish top of the course. With three and a half thousand budding lawyers at Monash I wasn't that good but I wasn't bottom either. I had given it my best shot and I now wanted to tell Grandpa that it was his encouragement that carried me through and I wanted him to attend my graduation ceremony. Of course I wanted my Mum and Dad to be there also. But I thought I owed it to Grandpa to tell him personally what his support meant to me. I wanted to let him know that he was special.

When I knocked on his door I had to wait a few seconds for him to get up from his chair come down the hall and unlock the door. Grandpa was in his nineties and just a little less spritely than he had been seventy years before. He didn't say anything when he saw me standing there. All he did was throw his arms around me, hug me like no one else ever did and pull me into the house. There was no other grandpa like my grandpa.

When we were seated and I told him why I had come to see him he said, "I wondered if you would come, Grandson." He nearly always called me grandson. "The wildest brumbies in this fair land of ours wouldn't keep me away. And let me tell you here and now, I am proud of you. You are the first lawyer in the family and I hope you will rise to great heights. The law is a worthy profession and will be for you what you make of it. But remember this, learned though you may be in law your learning will not stand alone. The only reason for law is that we might all know where we are in the scheme of things and so that justice may be done. Sometimes, strange though it may seem, the law gets in the way of justice."

"I often hear people say that discretion should be taken away from magistrates and judges and that sentencing should be mandatory. That's bunkum, Grandson, in my opinion. In law, I think, that what is needed is more discretion in the people who sit with great power in their hands. Those people sit with the power to make or break a person and wreck a family. It is a great burden. Life is not about black and white law. Life is about people. People are what counts in life and they must be treated with kindness, care and courtesy. Grandson, those people who place their trust in you depend on you to do what is right no matter what."

And then Grandpa said, "Fiat Justitia Ruat Caelum." I was

amazed. I looked at him in astonishment. He returned my look with a chuckle. "You didn't think your old grandfather knew Latin, did you?"

"No, I didn't Grandpa."

"Well, you are quite correct, I don't. I learned that phrase just so that I could see the look on your face when I quoted it to you. You young lawyers needn't think that you are the bee's knees who can chuck little bits of a long dead language about and bamboozle the poor unknowing peasants. Now, do you know what it means?"

"Yes I do: Let justice be done though the heavens fall."

"Bravo. I would have been surprised and disappointed if you hadn't known. That phrase has a long history in jurisprudence not only in Australia but throughout the world. I often think of it in connection with the matter I want to talk to you about. You know about the case of Cass Carrington?"

It was more of a statement than a question. He was correct. I did know. If there was any person in Australia who hadn't heard of R v Carrington then they must have been sleep-walking all of their lives. It was the story of a great love, a great scandal and a great disgrace.

So I was delighted to be able to say, "Yes, of course I have, Grandpa. Who hasn't? I know about your part in it though I have never heard you talk about it. It's about that strange wrinkle in the criminal law that allows a person who may be guilty to escape the consequences of their alleged crime. We rehashed that case again and again in our criminal tutorials at uni. Our group was split fairly evenly on whether justice had been done or not. I still find it hard to come to terms with. Had the case been tried by a judge sitting alone then the outcome would, undoubtedly, have been different. Purists use the case as an illustration of just how flawed the jury system is."

"Cruel though it may seem, Grandpa, I am inclined to agree with them. The law is the law and the law should be obeyed. Otherwise what's the point? To me it is only right that someone who on the face of it has committed murder, no matter who they are or what they are or how exemplary their life may have been up to then, should pay for their crime. It seems so contrary to justice that a person who has committed and been charged with murder can walk away unpunished just because twelve good men and women can't make up their minds or don't want to make up their minds. At uni, Grandpa, we were taught that homicide is the killing of a human being by a human being with malice aforethought express or implied. In Carrington's case there was abundant evidence to illustrate beyond a reasonable doubt that Carrington had malice aforethought sufficient to prove his guilt. Yet it seems to that the jury system was sadly lacking. The law might have been complied with but where did that leave justice? How can any right-thinking member of society say that justice was done in that case?"

"That's why I wanted to talk to you, Grandson. You talk, Grandson, with the great and certain clarity of youth. The problem is that as we get older things do not seem so black and white. The law is so black and white you might think that by following it it would be easy to make a decision. But, no, justice is a horse of a different colour. Sometimes, in the courts, justice is done and sometimes it isn't. Let me tell you the full story and then ask you what you would have done if you had been one of the jury members involved. It'll take a little time. Would you like to hear it?"

I could see that grandpa dearly wanted me to say yes so I said, "Yes I do, Grandpa."

"In that case make yourself comfortable, sit back and listen and I'll set the whole matter before you. When I have finished you can tell me what you think of the whole process as any good lawyer would under the Audi Alteram Partem rule. My goodness, there I go again, quoting Latin. He gave another chuckle."

Grandpa was enjoying himself. I didn't have to ask what the rule he had just quoted meant. It means, hear the other side.

CHAPTER TWO

It all started rather a long time ago, Ben, well before you were born. It was the 1940s and the world was in turmoil. A crazy man in Germany had set the world alight and millions were to die before the world regained its sanity, if it ever did.

Here in Melbourne we should have all felt very safe because we were far away from the bedlam that was Europe. But we weren't. We were tied to England's apron strings and where the Poms went Australia went. I was young and unknowing and the glory of war drew me like a magnet. I wanted to be out there fighting the angry Hun and winning medals to show how brave I was. All part of the folly of youth. I was to find before I was much older that I was not as brave as I thought. Sometimes I quaked with fear. But you won't tell on me, will you?

"No, I won't, Grandpa. Not ever."

Good lad! Let's get on.

I was at the base training camp when I met Cassidy Ambrose Carrington. As we Aussies are wont to do we shortened his first name to Cass and to all of us even when he became sergeant he was still Cass. He and I were billeted in the same hut. His bed was right next to mine so we became closer than we might otherwise have been.

I was at the side of my bed unpacking my suitcase when he came up beside me.

"Is this bed taken?" he asked, pointing at the empty bed beside mine.

"Not as far as I know. I don't think they reserve beds here."

"This will do for me. Do you mind if I join you?"

"Not at all. Make yourself at home. My name's Jarrad Bruce but everybody calls me Rad," and I put out my hand.

He put his hand into mine, a good firm grasp and said, "I'm Cassidy."

He looked me directly in the face as we shook. I returned his gaze and saw myself looking at a tall thin man with a long face. It was a white face. So very white that I wondered if he had been ill. But then I thought he couldn't have been that ill or they wouldn't have had him in the army although at that time getting into the army wasn't difficult. Cannon-fodder was in great demand. And when I say he was thin I mean very thin. He looked to me like he hadn't eaten for weeks. In Oz there was then, as there is now, plenty of food and plenty of sunshine. So how come he was so pale and thin? A funny thought struck me but I cast it quickly from my mind because it seemed so unfair - I wondered if he had been in jail. That pallor just wasn't natural. Not in an Aussie. Then I thought to myself some people are naturally thin and maybe he has worked indoors a lot. Anyway, it was none of my business. He seemed like a decent guy and I was never curious enough to stick my nose into other people's business. If he and I were together long enough I was sure I would find out all about him.

As I unpacked he stood watching me.

"Where's your luggage?' I asked.

"He put his hand in his pocket and drew out a safety razor and a toothbrush and placed them in the drawer of the little locker at the side of his bed."

"That's my luggage. I always travel light."

"I wish I could travel like that," I said. I thought I had embarrassed him so I changed tack and said, "Where you from?"

He looked at me for a moment before he replied, "Oh, I

7

came from the sticks. Not quite beyond the black stump, but nearly. I come from Narrogin."

"Never heard of it," I said. "Where is it?"

He didn't seem in the least put out by my ignorance. In fact he seemed pleased.

"It's a little country town about one hundred and twenty miles (about 200 km) on the other side of Perth. I'm not surprised you haven't heard of it. It's a rather sleepy little place. Nobody has ever heard of Narrogin. Nothing ever happens there."

"I suppose that's why you're here?"

"Not exactly but that will do." Then he turned the subject back to me. "Where are you from?"

"I'm from the city to beat all cities. I'm from marvellous Melbourne and it's not sleepy. It is the best city in Australia. It has to be good. It was called after an English lord as I'm sure you already know?"

"Yeah, I know that. I've never lived in such a big city. I suppose it's easy to get lost there?"

"No, you would never get lost in Melbourne. All you have to do is catch a tram and it will take you back where you started out from. But you don't have to worry if you ever want to go to Melbourne. You just have to say so and I'll be your guide. I'll show you where the most beautiful girls in Australia live."

"I've never been on a tram. I'd like that. But if Melbourne's so great why are you here? Why did you leave it?" And he smiled a smile that lighted up that pale face of his.

"Well you know, some of us are never content. We get bored after a while no matter where we are. The truth is I just wanted to see the world. I thought the army was a cheap way to do it. The way things are going I can see us getting a free ride to Europe before too long."

"You're not wrong there. But what a ride it will be."

We were friends from that moment. We were friends ever after. And he was a good mate. The best mate I ever had.

CHAPTER THREE

Some things made me wonder about him. Even when a group of us would be sitting around chewing the fat he didn't seem to be able to let himself go. Always he was guarded, defensive. I just couldn't understand it then but he always seemed lonely to me. He didn't go out a lot; he didn't mix a lot. He didn't talk much but he listened a lot. It seemed to me that he preferred not to be asked about his background. If it ever came up he would make some non-committal reply and change the subject. On one occasion when a group of us were having a beer in the canteen and the subject turned to girls and sex as it always did Cecil Wilson said, "I used to be madly in love with a girl from Narrogin, Cass. Man she was something else. I still dream about her. Narrogin being a small town and all you might know her. She was called Kate Dexter."

Cass looked at him for a moment, seemed to reflect before saying, "Can't say as I have, Cec. Narrogin isn't that small, you know. If you were so madly in love with her why do you talk about her in the past tense?"

The subject was turned back on Cec.

"I don't know, Cass. One day it seemed she loved me to distraction and the next I was yesterday's man. I was broken-hearted for at least a week when she didn't turn up for our next date. When I went to her house to enquire about her it was her father who answered the door. He didn't seem pleased to see me. He said I wasn't a man of honour and to get lost or he'd sool the dog on me. He was holding the dog in his arms. It bared its teeth at me. It looked a real man-eater. It was one of those little poodle things. Frightened the wits out of me it did. I couldn't understand it. All I had done was put my hand on Kate's knee under her skirt up to the top of her silk stockings. I can tell you feeling that lovely skin of hers made the thrills run up and down my spine. I might even have got a bit excited. You see I had half a mind, maybe more than half a mind, to see the colour of her knickers just so I would know how they compared with mine, you understand?" And he looked at us with that droll look of his.

"Mine were pretty pink. I wondered what colour hers were. The comparison would have made a nice talking point. If they were the same colour as mine and even if they weren't we would have had something in common to talk about. I thought she liked my attempt at close personal contact. However I got the impression from her father's demeanour that she didn't and that somehow I had overstepped the mark. There was no doubt about it I had become persona non grata and I knew that if that dog ever got loose I was dog-meat. So I made myself scarce, at speed. Who understands women? I sure as hell don't. I just can't handle them. I know how to do the physical bits. At least I think I do but I'm just no good at chatting them up. I'm more the strong silent type. I'm never able to look deep into their eyes and whisper sweet nothings in their ears. I want to alright but I just can't do it. My tongue always sticks to the roof of my mouth when I want to say something romantic. I decided there and then to join the French Foreign Legion and give women away. The trouble was I didn't know how to get in touch with the Frogs and anyway there was a war on and the Frogs didn't seem to be doing too well so I opted for the Australian army. I thought maybe if the war took me to Paris and I did something brave I might become a hero and then some Paris dolly-bird might take pity on me and show me the colour of her lingerie and maybe want to bond with me. But the only thing famous about me is that I'm a coward and I don't see any hope of any female under seventy, or maybe over it for that matter, wrapping her legs around me and offering me her all. Life just isn't fair. And now I'm in the army and the only one to love me is the company sergeant major. I think he's attracted to my salmon pink underpants."

Cec hooted with laughter then. We all did.

Cec was like that. He talked with a dead straight face and an intimate mournful voice as if he was deadly serious but underneath it all he laughed at life.

I was watching Cass during this exchange. He seemed relieved that the conversation had been taken over by Cec.

CHAPTER FOUR

One of the things that amazed me at that time about Cass was his appetite. On that first day when we went to the mess hall for our first meal as soldiers and sat side by side at the dining-table I could hardly believe what I was seeing. He had cleaned his plate before I was half way through mine. It was as if he hadn't seen food for a week. He went for seconds and had that cleared just as I finished my first. A third plateful and he was still licking his lips. And they were all heaped plates. The desserts had the same treatment. Three platefuls. Yet he still looked as if he could have done the same again. It wasn't that he half cleared any plate either. Each one when he was finished with it was as near to being polished as it ever would be. For every meal it was the same. During all the time I spent with him I never once heard him complain about the food. Some of our mates would grumble about how bad the food was and long for a meal cooked by their mothers. Cass never grumbled no matter what. He just cleaned up everything. On one occasion I said to him, "You're not pregnant, are you, Cass?"

"He looked at me surprised. "What do you mean?" he asked.

"It always seems that you are eating for two."

He gave one of those quiet laughs of his. "No, Rad, I'm not pregnant. It's just that I suffer from deep ingrained insecurity. The last time I saw my shrink he said I had the camel mentality, that eating was my way of satisfying all my latent desires. He said that I had to be careful and to come back to him if ever it appeared that I was getting a hump on my back."

And so he laughed off my enquiry.

Another thing I noticed about him in our first days at the camp was that after a day's drilling, square-bashing or work-outs in the gym he would come back to the billet, throw himself on the bed and be asleep in an instant. It was as if he had no energy. Yet, not once did he complain. No matter what the army threw at him he took it with a martyr-like, dogged determination and said nothing. It was almost as if he had something to prove.

When it came to square-bashing he was way ahead of the rest of us and he handled a rifle as if he had been born with one in his hand. On that first day on the square the drill sergeant said to him, "You there, soldier. Have you done this before?"

Cass seemed taken aback and it took him a few seconds to reply. "No, Sergeant. I haven't."

"Looks to me like you have. The way you handle that rifle tells me you've handled one before."

For a moment Cass seemed knocked out of kilter but he recovered himself quickly and said, "I'm sorry to say, Sarge, you've got it wrong. But I was a non-commissioned officer in the Salvation Army. The drill sergeant there was very strong on discipline and took a shine to me. He let me carry the flag on ceremonial occasions. I think if I had stayed there I might have got a commission."

"I might have known it," said the sergeant. "Every squad has a comedian or a smart ass. I can forgive you for that but you can't be forgiven for telling your sergeant that he's got it wrong. That is usually a hanging rap. Your sergeant is never wrong. Now, for your bravery and your big mouth you can put your rifle above your head and double round this square three times. That'll teach you when you are asked a sensible question to give a sensible answer."

Cass put his rifle above his head and ran.

Although he was good at drill he always seemed to have trouble with his salute. Instead of putting his hand up to the side of his head with the palm outwards his hand always went to the middle of his right eyebrow with the palm inwards. Time after time he was caught out. Some of the young officers got worked up about it and put him on report. It took months for him to get it right. But it was a case of swings and roundabouts. Because he was so good at what he did and always went at soldiering as if his life depended on it and never held a grudge against any of the officers who gave him a hard time, we all admired him. He never bragged, he never boasted. To me he was a decent quiet dependable guy. I liked him very much and wished I could soldier like him.

I remember looking at him one day after we had been at the camp for about three months and wondering at the change in him. He had put on weight, was no longer deathly pale and had energy to spare. In the marathon cross-country races he was now always up with the leaders and no longer dragged himself in with the end stragglers. It was almost as if he was a new man. And he no longer ate quite so much though he still had a healthy appetite.

Came the end of our basic training and we were granted two week's home leave. I couldn't wait to get home to Melbourne to show off my new uniform to my Mum and Dad and my sister Elsie. Then, too, Elsie was getting married and had put the ceremony off so that I could be her groom's man in my dress uniform. I couldn't help talking about it. Cass listened to me patiently day after day though I must have been a bore.

"It looks like you're going to have a good time, Rad. Must be wonderful to have a family like that."

It was the first time he had ever mentioned family and I felt just a little bit embarrassed. I had talked all about my plans for my leave and never asked him about his. For a few seconds there was a gap in our conversation and I didn't know what to say. I knew I had to say something, but what?

Then I said, "What about you, Cass? I suppose you are heading for Narrogin?"

"I don't think so. I'm not sure what I'm doing. I haven't made up my mind yet."

"Why don't you come home with me and I'll show you around Melbourne. I'm sure Mum and Dad would love to meet my best mate. What about it?"

He was reluctant at first but in the end said he thought it was a great idea as long as he wasn't going to be a trouble.

"No trouble at all. It'll be great to have you."

CHAPTER FIVE

I didn't know then what that invitation would lead to. If I had I think I would have left him to go his own way. But that's hindsight. He was my mate and I was trying to look after him.

The first thing I did when we arrived at the train station in Melbourne was to walk across the street and grab a tram.

"There you are," I said. "You're on a Melbourne tram at last. What do you think of it?"

"I like it. Maybe after the wedding we can spend a day riding the rails. It would be a good way to see Melbourne."

"We'll do that. There's a lot of Melbourne to see and I can't think of better way of doing it than sitting in a tram."

"After our tram trip we can drop off at Young and Jackson's in Flinders Street and have a yard of beer. It'll settle the dust in our throats after all that square bashing. We can forget about the army for a couple of weeks."

"That, Rad, sounds like a good idea to me."

We got off the tram a couple of streets from my home and we almost ran the last few metres to the front door. But we didn't get to the door. It suddenly burst open and there was Mum and Dad and Elsie racing up the street to meet us. They must have been standing at the window waiting for us to turn the corner. The three of them wanted to grab me at the same time. I felt like a king at that moment and was almost overcome with emotion. That was one of the happiest days of my life. I so much wanted Cass to see how much they loved me.

My father was the first to stop hugging me. Turning to Cass he put out his hand and said, "I'm sorry, Cass, we are a bit like this in our family. We get carried away at times. I know you're Cass. Rad has told us all about you. You're very welcome. Come inside and make yourself at home."

"Not before he has given me a hug," said my mother.

"And me too," said Elsie.

They both flung their arms around him at the same time. Poor Cass. He was overwhelmed. But that was my family. We were nothing if not extroverts.

And Cass loved it.

In the middle of all the hugging my Mum said to my sister, "Go easy, Elsie. You don't want to frighten the poor lad away. He must wonder what's he's got himself into. And anyway, you don't want Rob to hear you've been hugging another man in the street, do you?"

"Rob won't mind in the least. He knows he's got me right where I want him", laughed Elsie.

And that was Cass's introduction to our family.

CHAPTER SIX

The wedding was a great success. Cass said he had never been to a wedding before and didn't realise how much he had missed.

"You can't beat a wedding, Cass," said my mother. "You never know, the next one might be yours," she quipped.

Cass was ever so slightly embarrassed. He didn't reply, just shuffled his feet and looked at the floor.

I think my mother did it deliberately and had matchmaking in mind. I was convinced of that when at the reception she arranged for Cass to be seated next to Katharine Carr. Katharine was never called Katharine; to us she was always Kitty.

Kitty was one of Elsie's best friends. A little brown mouse of a girl, she was very quiet, very self-effacing, happy to be part of the crowd but hardly ever had anything to say for herself. And as far as I know had never had a boyfriend. She was just too shy. When I looked at her and Cass sitting side by side I wondered who would break the ice first. What happens when two good listeners meet? Does one suddenly find that they have just become a good conversationalist? Had Mum overstepped the mark? I was sitting at the top table where the bride and groom were sitting and with all the hubbub going on around me I couldn't hear what Cass and Kitty were saying but I could see them clearly and I was surprised. They seemed to be in animated conversation. Kitty's cheeks were flushed and her eyes shining. She wasn't a little brown mouse anymore. Kitty had come alive. She was leaning close to Cass as if it was important that she catch his every word. And her wine glass was almost empty. Elsie had always told me how it was that Kitty would never drink anything other than soft drinks. I think that before that night she had never tasted alcohol. And Cass looked as if he was a different person too. He who was always so reserved, so lonely, so quiet, now looked as if an inner light had been lit. I was looking at a Cass I had never seen before. I was glad then that I had brought him home.

The next day when I said, "Would you like to go for that tram-ride round Melbourne, Cass?", I was amazed when he said, "I would, Rad, but I hope you don't mind. Kitty has volunteered to show me the sights of this great city of yours. She has taken the whole day off work for that purpose."

"By heaven, it didn't take you long. Go for it." And there I was thinking you were slow.

He chuckled. "I'm not as slow as you might think."

And that was the start of the world's greatest romance. Every day for the rest of our leave he went out with Kitty. He would go to her place of work at lunch-time and when she came out they would go off arm in arm to some quiet spot or other and eat sandwiches together. He would leave her back at the office door. In the evening when she finished work he would be back again. They'd be off on a tram and that was them until the next day and the next day when they did the same all over again. Our family was delighted. None more than me. We couldn't stop talking about it. Mum said, "You know, Rad, I think those two will tie the knot before you know it. They appear to me to be madly in love. And the thing is she is half way there already. All she has to do is to add ington to Carr and she's his."

"You're getting carried away, Mum. A couple of days back at the camp and he'll have forgotten all about her. This is a summer storm. It's just too full on to last."

"Don't be so sure. Just wait and see."

I did wait and I did see. I could do nothing else. Mum was right. Women's intuition won the day.

On the day that Cass and I set out to return to the camp Mum and Dad and Kitty left us at the train. Elsie was off on her honeymoon with Bob. Mum and Dad hugged and kissed me and I gave Kitty a peck on the cheek. Then it was Cass's turn. Mum and Dad both put their arms around him and told him that they were glad that I had him for a mate and that he could come to our place any time.

"I know you'll both look out for each other," said my father, "And we'll look after Kitty for you," said my mother with a knowing look at me. When it came to Cass and Kitty saying goodbye they went into a clinch I thought was going to cause us to miss our train. I threw our things, his and mine through the door and followed them in. The train was beginning to move off when the clinch was broken and Cass jumped on board. Then he hung out the door window waving until the train went round the bend and they were out of sight. I remember Kitty shouting as the train pulled away, "I'll write to you every day, Cass." And his reply, "And I'll write to you, Kitty." Then we were both sitting side by side with our heads back and not a word between us for several minutes. When Cass spoke it was to say, "That was the best holiday I've ever had, Rad. Thank you for it."

"I'm glad you liked it. I knew you were enjoying it. For a while I thought I wasn't going to get you back. You were so caught up with Kitty I thought you were going to go AWOL."

He laughed then. "You don't know how nearly right you are, Rad. I did think about it but commonsense prevailed. What would I have done if I had chucked in the army? I don't think Kitty would have loved me if I had."

"I'm sure she would love you no matter what you did, Cass.

I think you have become her knight in shining armour. Some guys have all the luck and here I am like Cec Wilson, with the company sergeant major the only one to love me."

We both laughed at that.

CHAPTER SEVEN

The break did us both a world of good. It certainly made a changed man out of Cass. More than ever did he throw himself into being a soldier like no other. What I think he wanted was to make Kitty proud of him. He knew that I would be writing home and telling my Mum and Dad how well he was doing and that my Mum would be sure to tell Kitty. He was as good as his word. He wrote to Kitty every day and she wrote to him. Before, when the mail was delivered, he took no interest. I wondered about that, too. Had he no one who cared about him? No one to write to him or for him to write to? That kind of thing would surely make a man lonely. But he was lonely no more. He could hardly wait for the mail to arrive. Every day there was a letter for him except for Wednesdays then he received three letters. Obviously Kitty had written to him on Friday, Saturday and Sunday and he received the three letters together. He would take his letters and go off to read them on his own. When he would reappear his face would be shining. It was clear to me that Cass had found his heaven. I envied him. I would have liked to be in love like that. I would dearly have loved to read one of those letters but that was a very private thing between him and Kitty and I couldn't ask except to enquire how she was. He never volunteered anything other than that she was fine.

Our next leave was coming up soon when one Wednesday after he had received his three letters he came to me and said, "Rad, there's something I'd like to run past you. Can we go somewhere quiet and talk?"

I said, "Sure. Let's go for a wander on the other side of the parade ground. Nobody will interfere with us there."

He said nothing till we were well away from everyone else. Then he hit me with his bombshell. "Rad, I've asked Kitty to marry me and I've got her reply back today. She has said she thought I would never ask - what took me so long?"

He got no further. I took his right hand in both of mine and said, "Congratulations, Cass. I'm delighted for you. You don't let the grass grow under your feet, do you? Now, what's your problem?"

"Well it's just that I don't know where to get married or how to organize it."

I laughed with sheer joy then. "Cass, you have no problem. You can be married from our place. My Mum and Dad will be delighted. My Mum just loves a wedding. How does that grab you?"

"It grabs me very well. But how do you know what your Mum and Dad will say?"

"I know very well. I'll write to them as soon as we get back to billet and get it set it up. All you have to do is write to Kitty and tell her that she will be Mrs Carrington before her next birthday and that she will be married in Melbourne in the same church where Elsie was married. That'll make it easy for you both. You'll know your way about. You both being a bit slow and all."

He laughed at that.

"There's one other thing I'd like to ask, Rad. Would you be my best man?"

"If you hadn't asked I would never have spoken to you again. You can bet your sweet life I will. Anything else troubling you?"

"Nothing, Rad. Thanks for being a good mate."

And so it was all settled as easy as that.

CHAPTER EIGHT

Kitty had a girl from her office as her bridesmaid and I was once again the groom's man. They were married on a day when the sun shone out of an azure blue sky such as only Melbourne can lay on. The weather certainly was on their side. For once we didn't have four seasons in one day. A horse and carriage took Cass and his new wife to the hotel where the reception was held. My Mum and Dad paid for the drinks and because he was a soldier and there was a war on the hotel shouted them and any of the guests who wanted it free accommodation for the night. There was little need for accommodation for some of the guests who drank into the wee small hours. Cass and Kitty slipped off early in the morning to their secret honeymoon location. Even I didn't know where they went.

The next I saw of him was when he arrived back at the camp. When I saw him I just couldn't resist it. I said, "You alright, Cass? You look completely worn out to me. Poor fellow, it looks as if that wife of yours has made things hard for you."

He smiled at that. "You know, Rad, I nearly didn't come back. It seems that I haven't lived up to now. The worst part is now. Kitty's there and I'm here. I dunno how I'm going to do without her."

"Don't worry about that," I said. "Get her up here. Surely you'll be able to find a place for her in town where you can see her every night. Life is for living Cass. Tonight you and I will go into the town and see what we can find."

"Would you, Rad? Would you? It would be wonderful if I could have Kitty here."

That same evening we went into town and searched around until we found a real estate agency. We arrived at the door just as a girl was putting the key in the lock to lock up for the day. We introduced ourselves and I told her we were looking for a place for my mate's wife to stay as they had only just been married and she wanted to see a little of her husband before he was moved overseas. The lady said she understood, took the key out of the door, smiled and said, "Come inside. This might be your lucky day. I think I have just the place for you."

We followed her inside. I hardly dared breathe. Could it be that we had hit the jack-pot at our first attempt? The lady asked us both to be seated then went to a desk, opened a drawer and drew a folder from it. "This just came in this morning. We haven't had time to advertise it yet," she said. "The thing is it's furnished. And when I say furnished I mean totally furnished. Did you want a furnished place?" and she looked at Cass with her eyebrows raised. "If you do this is the place for you."

"That's exactly what I want," said Cass. "Tell me about it."

The lady smiled then went into a sales pitch like you wouldn't believe. She didn't know it but she had no need. Cass and I were already away ahead of her.

"This was the house of old Mrs Rafferty who lived here for years after her husband died. She has passed away recently and the family are anxious that the house not be left unoccupied whilst they await probate. Obtaining probate may take months. The family live in Sydney and what with one thing and another would be willing to let the premises at a very reasonable rental until such times as they have things sorted out. I'm confident that you won't have a better offer than this anywhere in this area. And, of course, it is close to the army camp. What do you think?"

"How much is the rent?" I was trying hard to keep the quaver out of my voice.

When she told us I thought she was having us on. I thought there must be some other hidden expense but I was wrong. I was afraid to speak in case my voice gave the game away. Cass couldn't speak either.

She looked at us both for a moment, got the wrong impression and said, "There's nothing wrong with the house. You are getting a bargain. The rent is so low because what the family really want is a kind of caretaker. I assure you that if you take this place you will have no regrets. I'm sure the family would be happy that a serving soldier's wife has it."

It was Cass who spoke first. He had recovered more quickly than I had. I had thought I must be dreaming. "I'll take it," he said. Do you want a deposit now?"

That the lady was genuine was apparent from what she said next.

"Before you commit yourself I think it would be better if you held off until you have seen what you're letting yourself in for. What I'll do is I'll speak to the landlord and let you know. I can't see any problem. I will then do any necessary paperwork and have the whole thing set up so that when you come tomorrow all you will have to do is sign the lease agreement, pay the deposit and the place is yours. Can you come tomorrow about the same time?"

"Yes, we can come tomorrow," acquiesced Cass.

"Good. If all is to your satisfaction and the landlord's by this time tomorrow you should be in possession of the best bargain you are ever likely to meet in this sweet life of ours," and she laughed. "With a little bit of luck, Mr Carrington, your wife could be here within the week."

She then picked up the folder and walked us to her car. A ten minute drive and we were in a side street and outside a little three bedroom house standing on its own grounds with a garden front and back. There were orange, lemon, plum and cherry trees in the back garden. And it was only five minutes walk from the camp. As we walked up the three steps to the front door I couldn't help admiring the roses in the little border that fringed the veranda. They were red, white and yellow and were just beautiful. The whole place had a welcoming feel about it. Cass and I didn't really need to go inside. We were sold already but we didn't like to make it too obvious in case the agent decided that the rent was too low.

"There were two single bedrooms and one double. The double one had a large queen-size bed in it." There was a fan on a little table at the end of the bed. I looked at it and couldn't resist saying, "After you get Kitty here, Cass, you'll be glad of that fan. I can see hot and steamy nights ahead."

Cass only chuckled but didn't say anything. I think he didn't want to embarrass the sales lady. She said nothing but she did smile knowingly.

CHAPTER NINE

I knew the moment I saw it that this was the place for Cass and Kitty. And it had everything: kettles, saucepans, pots and pans, cutlery, all kinds of tableware, blankets and sheets. I noticed too that it had a dog-door cut in the laundry door. I thought to myself, I bet it won't be long before there is a dog in this house to come in and go out through that door. So far as Cass was concerned it was a dream. All Kitty had to do was to bring herself up from Melbourne, unlock the door and she was at home.

After our tour of inspection the lady ran us back to the camp. We exited the car and said we would see her next day. As she drove off down the road Cass and I hugged each other. "I think this is your lucky day, Cass," I said. "If we get that place Kitty will love it."

"Oh, she'll love it," he said. "I already love it. I only hope that we get it."

The next day we were back at the real estate office. Cass signed the papers, paid the deposit, took possession of the keys and we were on our way. We didn't waste a minute but went straight back to the house and really went through it. It was spotless. I could see that Cass was very pleased. No wonder. If he had had a thousand houses to pick from he couldn't have picked a better one. It had such a warm cosy feeling about it. It was almost as if the house had put its arms around him and hugged him. I have never seen a man as happy as Cass was at that moment. His face was glowing and he was almost breathless with excitement. He didn't have to say anything; the look on his face said it all. He had found his little bit of heaven. It's a pity that such moments are so transient.

We left the house running and made it to the camp post office a bare couple of minutes before closing time so that Cass could send off a telegram to Kitty to tell her to drop everything, pack her bags, get the next bus and join her husband pronto. Cass's hands were shaking as he wrote out that telegram. Next morning he had a reply telegram from Kitty telling him that she was on her way. Only then did it suddenly hit him that he hadn't told the army authorities what he had done.

That caused something of a kerfuffle in the army administration but everybody was very good and things got sorted out though it took a little time. One of the things that Cass had to have sorted out very quickly was permission to spend his nights at home with his wife. He had to appear before his commanding officer and explain how it was that he had not followed army rules and ask for permission before he acted. The commanding officer was a strict disciplinarian but he was a good man and when he heard Cass say that he had to strike while the iron was hot otherwise he would have missed a good bargain he understood. He listened patiently with a little smile flickering about his face as he saw Cass trying hard to justify his acting outside the rules. In the end the CO said, "I'll make an exception in this case, Carrington but only because there is a war on. One thing I want to make clear to you and other like-minded personnel is should it happen that your conjugal duties conflict with your army requirements then I will most certainly revoke these arrangements. We can't have a soldier reporting for early morning duty in a state of extreme exhaustion. Is that understood?"

"Yes, sir."

"Good. Application approved."

Cass was out of there like a shot. First thing he did when he got back to his billet was to ask me what conjugal meant. I didn't know either. We both found a dictionary and looked it up. When we found the answer we both roared with laughter. The CO had a sense of humour.

CHAPTER TEN

I accompanied Cass to the bus stop to meet Kitty. I didn't really want to go but he insisted.

"I'll need you there, Rad, to help with her luggage. After we get her home you won't need to stay." He looked at me then with a knowing look. "But I do want you there."

And so I agreed. He wanted to do things in style and cut a bit of a dash. So after we had travelled into the town on the army bus he engaged a taxi to be waiting at the bus station. Standing outside the taxi waiting for Kitty's bus to arrive he could not stand still. He kept walking up and down and looking at his watch. He would run to look at every bus that came into the station and wait to see if it was the right one. After what seemed like a fortnight, actually it was only thirty six and a half minutes, a bus came in. There she was sitting in the front seat nearest the door. As the door opened and she reached the step nearest the ground he ran forward, threw his arms around her and whirled her on to the ground all the while smothering her face with kisses.

A rather plump lady passenger, who looked to be in her sixties, who was immediately behind Kitty, stepped out of the bus and said to the man meeting her, "Now why can't you greet me like that?" "I was just about to but I have a touch of arthritis in both arms. Just give me a second and I'll do the best I can. I have to watch the flying feet of that lucky lady in front of you." "You haven't changed a bit. Always excuses, excuses, excuses." She laughed as he hugged her.

The bus driver came out from his cabin, opened the luggage compartment and pulled out the cases. Kitty had three. I think those three cases contained all her worldly goods. The taxi driver and I put them in the boot of the taxi while Cass stood with arms around Kitty kissing her and holding her like he didn't want to stop. I knew then why he was so keen to have me accompany him. The taxi-driver nudged me and whispered, "Is this guy always like this?"

"Most of the time," I replied. "You should see him when he gets excited."

Cass and Kitty had just about brought life at the bus station to a standstill. It wasn't my fault. I had nothing to do with it. Everybody standing around had broad grins on their faces.

Cass and Kitty got into the back seat. I got into the front and we took off. The back seat passengers did not see any of the passing scene, they were too busy about other things. At the house Cass and Kitty got out arm in arm. The driver helped me carry the cases and put them on the veranda. I opened the front door. Cass picked Kitty up in his arms, carried her up the steps on to the veranda, turned his back to the door to push it a little further open then carried his bride through into their first home.

I thought it was time for me to make myself scarce. I followed the driver to the door of his cab and said, "How much?" He looked at me with a wide grin and said, "Mate, I have carried many people in this old wagon of mine in the thirty years I have been driving but I have never witnessed anything like I have seen this day. Tell me, is it love, lust or lunacy?"

"It might be a mixture of all three. This is the first he has seen of his new wife since they were married just about three months ago. I suppose you could call it a second honeymoon."

"Gawd, mate, it does me good to see it. It sure as hell is great to be young. Those two have made my day. I'll tell my wife when I get home. You never know, I might get lucky. Tell you what,

I'll shout him and his lovely bride this one. Tell them when he surfaces tomorrow that he must take things easy. You have to take love in measured doses otherwise it can become addictive and can be bad for your health. Come. Three's a crowd. I'll drop you back at the camp. At the moment you and I are surplus to requirements around here."

He dropped me off at the camp gate, shook my hand and drove off chuckling.

CHAPTER ELEVEN

I went to my billet. Cec Wilson, Danny Simmons, George Sanders and most of our close mates were waiting. They all wanted to know how things went. I gave them a complete account of the whole reunion. There was much laughing and many ribald jokes. Cec Wilson said, "You mean you didn't go into the house, Rad?"

"No, Cec. I didn't think I was needed just then."

"You're not wrong there," laughed Danny Simmons.

"I suppose the second thing he did when he got in there was take off his shoes," laughed George Sanders.

"Lust is not so easily satisfied," said Cec. "I'd think that would be the third or maybe even the fourth thing he would do. That would be the way of it if it was me. Some guys have all the luck. And here I am still with only the bloody company sergeant major to lust after me. Life just isn't fair."

We were soldiers and far from home.

I could hardly wait for the next morning and wondered if Cass would get back to the camp on time for early morning parade. I hoped he would. I didn't want his domestic arrangement revoked before it got started.

I needn't have worried. I was just lacing up my boots when he came striding through the hut door. He looked radiant. His face shone with happiness.

I told him what the taxi-driver had said. He was very pleased.

I said, "I was worried about you, Cass. I didn't think you'd make it in time."

"Oh, I'll always make it, Rad. Don't worry about that. I

would hate to let the CO down and Kitty would never forgive me if I stuffed up. Mind you, I nearly didn't make it."

"How was that?"

"Well, as I came racing out the front door I tripped over Kitty's suitcases and went flying off the veranda and landed in the garden. Luckily I landed on my feet. I'll need to polish my boots again before we go on parade."

"You mean Kitty's cases were out on the veranda all night?"

"That's right. Somehow they got forgotten about in the welter of things. When I picked myself up in the garden I ran back up the veranda steps, flung them through the door and legged it for the camp. Life has become very interesting all of a sudden."

We both laughed.

CHAPTER TWELVE

Things settled down after a few says. Cass was able take off for home most days after our army duties were done except on those occasions when he had guard duty. Sometimes I would take his guard duty for him. He promised that he would repay me when we were moved and he could no longer see Kitty every day. I told him that I didn't need to be repaid, just seeing him and Kitty so happy was reward enough for me.

One day he asked me where he thought he could get a dog. Kitty's birthday was coming up and he wanted to give her something to keep her company when he wasn't around. "After all we have a dog-door already provided and we might as well use it," he laughed. "I know she'd like a dog," he said. "But where do I get one?"

"That's a good question?"

I had no idea. We were soldiers. Looking for a dog was something far from my mind. I wondered who would know where we could find a dog. A local would know. But we didn't know any locals. Oh, yes, we did. The real estate lady. She might know. There was one way to find out. Cass and I went to see her.

"A dog?" she said, excitement and in amazement both in her voice at the same time. "You won't believe this but my next door neighbour said to me just last night that she has a pup she wants to find a good home for. It's a kelpie-cross. If you're interested I will run you there right now. She's just a couple of streets away."

She looked at us both with raised eyebrows.

Without the least hesitation Cass said, "Run us, and by the way, the house is wonderful."

She laughed and said, "It's wonderful to have satisfied customers. I told you you and your wife would be happy there. You will never find a better bargain."

An hour later we were at Cass's house with the cutest little four-legged heart-thief you have ever seen. As he climbed the steps to the front door Cass handed the pup to me and said, "Just leave me to do the talking." I had hardly time to reply before he was knocking on his own door. Kitty answered it with a quizzical look on her face.

"Good morning, milady. Are you Mrs Kitty Carrington?"

"I surely am," she laughed.

"In that case I'd like to introduce you to a friend of mine who is going to guard you, love you and look after you when your husband is away fighting the angry Hun." He flung his arms around her, kissed her, swung her round, then turning to me said, "My good sir, would you kindly introduce this lovely lady to the fur-coated Carrington acquisition."

I stepped forward and handed him the pup.

He took him from me and gently placed him in her arms. There were tears in Kitty's eyes which shone with happiness as she took the little dog in her arms and held him to her. The pup played his part on cue by immediately licking her face.

"Happy birthday, Mrs Carrington," said Cass.

"And from me too," I said.

"Come in. Come in. Why are you both standing out there?"

Hugging the dog she led us into the lounge room. When we were all seated she, still holding her birthday present and Cass with his arms around her, said, "What's his name, Cass?"

"As far as I know he hasn't got one yet," he replied.

"Well, I have one for him." Addressing the pup she said, "You look just like my husband. In fact I see a large family resemblance. My husband is an unpredictable rascal. I never know what he's going to get up to next, so, you, being a close relative of his, are obviously a rascal as well. From this day forth your name will be Raskal. I love you, Cass and I already love you, Raskal."

She kissed her husband and hugged her birthday present. On that day Kitty was in her heaven. She was not alone. Cass and Raskal were both with her.

CHAPTER THIRTEEN

"It was on that day that I realized just how wise Cass was. He knew that Kitty was alone all day when he was at the camp. He also knew that she would be even more alone when we were shipped out overseas so he had got ahead of the game. When he wasn't there she would have Raskal and that would keep her engaged. That he was right became evident in the seventy two days that they spent together before we got our marching orders.

Every day Kitty would take Raskal to the park. At first as a pup she carried him most of the way. Then as he grew bigger and stronger she would walk him there. Seldom did she put a leash on him except when safety required it and always she was teaching him. She taught him to sit, stay, beg, and die for his country. He was intelligent and he learned quickly. With a wave of her hand she would have him stop in his tracks. When Cass would come home in the evening she and Raskal would meet him at the door. There she would throw her arms around her husband and when he had kissed her she would signal to Raskal who would sit and hold out his paw. Cass would always shake it. The dog knew his mistress better than she knew herself. His eyes followed every move she made. When she and Cass sat down for a meal at the dining-table Raskal sat on the floor beside her. Occasionally, she would place a piece of bread on his nose and say,

"You may eat this piece of bun
But not until I've counted one
Then again it will not do
If you snap er I count two

Good dog. Good dog
One…two…three."

And at three Raskal would give his nose a flick, send the piece of bun flying into mid-air, lunge after it and catch it before it hit the floor. He always got a clap for that and another piece of bun for his obedience, restraint and cleverness. And he loved it in the park when Kitty threw the ball for him. He would run after it until Kitty was worn out throwing it. They would walk home, he without a leash because he was so obedient and would act instantly on Kitty's command. Once home he would flop on his blanket and have a doze until tea-time when his master came home. Some dogs have it good. When Cass wasn't there Raskal was and he filled her life for his mistress. For Cass and Kitty those seventy two days were the happiest of their lives.

Occasionally, I would be invited to come and spend an evening with them. On those evenings I learned what domestic bliss was. They lived for each other. Sometimes I would think it strange that Cass could spend his days with me and his other mates learning how to kill people against whom he had no grudge. People who had wives, mothers, fathers and sisters just like him. All day, like the rest of us, he would charge with a fixed bayonet at dummies of German soldiers and rip them to shreds, or batter them to a pulp with his rifle wielded as a blunt instrument. Or he would learn how to throw a hand grenade to gain maximum effect from its blast. He became adept in the use of all kinds of firearms, single shot and automatic, and how to kill a person with his bare hands. He was a fast learner. Only had to be shown something once and he had it. Then he would practise and practise at it until he had it off perfectly. To me it was clear that he still had something to prove. None of us was surprised or envious when he was made corporal. He was the

41

best at what we did. Yet in the evening he would go back to his wife and their dog and lead a life of domestic bliss. My mother might have contributed in some small way to his marital happiness but the Australian army tilted his life in an entirely different direction; it made a killer out of him. A very efficient and effective killer.

His domestic happiness was too good to last. One bright Tuesday morning came the word; we were shipping out. While the rest of us were delighted that at last we would have the chance to prove our worth Cass was not so enthusiastic. Undoubtedly he wanted to go too but just as undoubtedly he didn't want to leave Kitty. But he put a brave face on it. He told her that with a bit of luck the Germans would come to their senses and throw in the towel very soon. They must surely see that with the might of the rest of the world against them they had no chance. What he didn't seem to realize was that there is no reasoning with a lunatic. Hitler had around him a gathering of sycophants and megalomaniacs who knew that when the war ended with their defeat, as it surely would, they would all end up dancing their way out of this life at the end of a rope. They clung to their lunatic and he continued to lead his lemmings to the cliff. The war would be over only when Germany was a battered wreck. That was going to take some time. It would seem like a lifetime for both Kitty and Cass. Their separation was something neither wanted to face. But it had to be faced. Cass was a soldier and soldiers go to war. Was it not always thus? Aye, indeed, men must work and women must weep though the harbour bar be moaning.

The rumours were rampant within the camp. Nobody knew where we were going and the army wasn't telling. Some had it that we were going straight into Germany itself with clouds of paratroopers being dropped into Berlin followed by gliders with thousands of men taking on Jerry on his own soil. Others said we would land in Russia where we would help the Russians to throw the Germans back to where they came from. Most thought that was an idiotic idea. The Russians were doing very well and didn't need our help. France was the favourite pick. Cec Wilson was sure it was France and looked forward to liberating Paris with a rifle in one hand and the other clutching a delectable dish to his manly chest. The simple fact was none of us knew. We were being taken on a mystery tour and we would have to wait and see.

I learned a lot on that boat journey that took us straight from Sydney harbour to Belfast dock. Yes, it was to Northern Ireland that we were boated. We only learned where we were when the ship docked. Paraded on deck our commanding officer addressed us. He was short and to the point. He told us where we were and impressed upon us the fact that we would be guests there and that we must act like gentlemen at all times.

At first when we arrived I thought that the army was playing some kind of game. When I heard the locals speak I thought we were in Scotland. Their speech didn't seem Irish. They said Aye, and Naw to rhyme with law just like Scots people do instead of Yes and No. They spoke so quickly that I was generally three or more words behind when they came to the end of a sentence so that when I didn't reply immediately they looked at me strangely as if I was a bit slow. I was indeed slow as far as they were concerned. But we soon got used to it. We accepted that we were indeed in Northern Ireland and that was the way the people spoke. It was some kind of throwback from history when the Scottish people went to Northern Ireland in droves to seek a better life. I found it amusing when I would meet a local and say in our Aussie way, "How are you going?" to receive the reply,

"I'm rightly." or "I'm bravely." I had never heard that terminology before and I couldn't help but smile at it. It was certainly different.

"There are people here who will not love you", the CO said. "Act like the Aussies you are and you may find that you are made welcome by all. Act like idiots and we will all suffer. I promise you that any man who brings this company into disrepute will get no sympathy from me. Dismissed."

Poor Cass. He was seasick for a large part of the journey. If the ship gave the slightest wobble he was over the side. He couldn't eat although we all told him he had to keep his strength up. He tried manfully but it was no good. He gave up in the end. Sometimes he drank water but up that came as well. I felt sorry for him. The medics offered him anti-seasickness tablets but he refused them. I was surprised when he told the medic, not too politely, which was unusual for him, "Stick your tablets. I've tried them before. They don't work for me. If I take those and you stick round a couple of minutes I'll give them back to you."

He really did suffer. I wondered how he knew that the tablets wouldn't work. He had never mentioned to me at any time that he had any sea-going experience or any experience afloat that would give him such knowledge. At first Cec, Danny and George would tease him and sing:

"A life on the ocean wave
A home on the rolling deep
Where the scattered waters rave
And the winds their revels keep."

But when they came to see how sick he really was they stopped and tried to make amends. We all did what we could to make life more bearable for him. It was only then that I realized what a terrible illness sea-sickness can be for those afflicted by it.

All the while he became thinner and whiter and began to look like he had when we first met. And, just as he did when we first met, as soon as the ship docked he started to eat for two. Three plates of main course and three for his dessert were normal. I knew then that he would soon be back in form. Usually he wrote to Kitty every day. However on this voyage his letters were a lot fewer. When I said to him in the middle of all his wretchedness, "It's a bloody good job you didn't join the Royal Australian Navy, Cass. That would have killed you," he stared at me unblinking for a few seconds before he said, "You speak such words of wisdom, Rad. I should have met you sooner."

I didn't know what he meant by that then. I had nothing else to say in reply.

We were marched about twenty miles (about 30 kilometres) from the ship to a little market town where we spent the night. The CO said the march would do us good. Weeks lying around on the ship twiddling our thumbs had made us fat and lazy, the CO said. That was not good for us. What we needed was a little exercise so we would be more ready to meet the enemy when that day came. Hence the march. Several of our mates complained that the march had left them with blisters. The only one not to complain was Cass. He told me that he would have marched the length of Ireland if it meant he was off that bloody ship.

A rest overnight and next morning, stiff and sore from our previous march, we marched the eight miles (13 kilometres) to the camp outside the little village where we were to be billeted. Half a mile (about one kilometre) outside the village the company sergeant said, "Give them Waltzing Matilda, fellows. If nothing else it will let them know where we are coming from."

That was how we arrived at the camp, singing our heads off.

It was our best day since we had left Sydney. Somehow the word had got ahead of us and as we approached the village more and more people came out from their houses and lined our route. They clapped and cheered us like we were conquering heroes and us not yet having fired a shot in anger. I heard shouts of "Man you're quare fellows." It was the first time I had heard the word 'quare'. I didn't know what it meant. I came to know that it was the Irish equivalent of 'You're a good un'. "Stick your bayonets up Schicklegruber's nose" and other anti-Nazi hate slogans were flung at us with patriotic fervour as we passed. You know, of course, Grandson that they didn't say nose.

CHAPTER FOURTEEN

Grandpa was ever polite. Not for him was the use of crude language.

"Yes, Grandpa, I know. I'm sure they didn't."

"Thought you would," he chuckled as he continued.

We knew then that we were among friends.

We had a day confined to camp before we were let loose to explore this new land. Most of us had never been out of Australia before and we wondered what we had got ourselves into. Before we were permitted to leave the camp the CO addressed us. He reminded us that we were guests in this country and that we must always act like gentlemen. No matter what we must not let Australia down.

"What I want to impress upon you," he said, "is that not everyone here will love you. You are now in a divided country part of which is at war with Germany and part of which is not. The Irish republican Army may not love you, though as Aussies you may get a free pass. Should you run into trouble at any time do not act the hero; just disengage, make a strategic withdrawal, head back to camp and report the nature of the provocation to your sergeant major. Be aware of this: any man who disobeys this order will be confined to barracks for the remainder of our time here. Go and enjoy yourself. It may be the last chance you'll get before you go to do what you have been trained for. Dismissed."

The next day Cass and I were among the first out the camp gate. We couldn't get into the village fast enough.

We were surprised at how peaceful it seemed. It didn't look like there was a war on. It might have been Australia for all the signs there were of conflict. True, German bombers had unloaded in Belfast but that was far from the village which appeared to have continued as it always had since the beginning of time. It was comprised of two rows of houses and shops which looked across the street at each other. At night it was as black as pitch because there was a black-out so that German bombers wouldn't mistake it for a large city and blast it out of existence. It boasted two pubs, three little grocer shops, a butcher's, a draper's and a petrol pump and that was about the lot. To tell it to you straight, Grandson, it, at first, seemed to me to be just a dismal bloody little dump.

I said to Cass, "Does this place remind you of anywhere? There couldn't be anywhere else in the entire world like this. And to think I joined the army for this. I thought it might have reminded you of Narrogin."

"You know I'm not one to make comparisons, Rad, but in my expert opinion I would say that Narrogin is a heaving, thrusting, bustling metropolis compared to this place."

We were both wrong. The place took on a completely different complexion when we were marched to church the following Sunday. Everyone in church shook hands with us, moved over in their pews and made room for us. Afterwards outside the church they shook our hands again and invited us to come round for Sunday lunch with them. They were the most welcoming people ever. The minister preached a sermon about young men leaving all that was near and dear to them and going forth to fight the forces of evil. We all thought that we were ten metres tall. It was a wonderful feeling. And still we hadn't met the enemy. That meeting would come soon enough.

One thing that we were all agreed upon was the weather. It was bloody awful. The rain never seemed to stop. How the people remained so cheery I don't know. When I told the locals that there were some places in Australia that hadn't seen rain for months, even years, they thought I was having them on. Then there was the cold. It was a hard winter and the frost turned us into human icicles. I never experienced anything like it. For the first time in my life I saw snow. Big fat fluffy flakes drifted down upon us so that we had difficulty opening the doors of our huts in the morning. But the fun of it. Oh, the fun of it. We pelted each other with snowballs, built snowmen, and snowwoman too. I won't tell you how we demonstrated the difference but we were soldiers, we were young and we loved to shock. Some of us even lay down in the snow and rolled in it. Snow was something to write home about.

CHAPTER FIFTEEN

One Saturday late in the afternoon Cass and I and a couple of mates were in the village. Some kids had thrown buckets of water down the main street and made a long slide. They didn't have skates, just boots or shoes. They would come running, hit the slide first with one foot, then the second, go down on their haunches and slide to the end. Just to see them was exhilarating. To see those young faces, orange pink with cold and glistening with the excitement of it all is something I shall never forget. After watching the kids for a while Cass took a long loping run and launched himself at the slide. For a moment I thought he wasn't going to make it because of the icy run up to it. Then he steadied himself, got both feet just the right distance apart and went gliding gracefully to the other end. I followed him and soon all our mates were at it. All went well until Jim Casey took a run, didn't judge it correctly, went head over tip, hit the ground with a crack and ended up with a broken wrist. Even that didn't stop the fun. He was hurried off to the doctor, his arm put in a sling and soon he was back cheering us on. Life was too short to moan and groan.

We began to enjoy the village and almost forgot there was a war on. The village has nothing but pleasant memories for me except for one incident which reminded us of what the CO had said. All was not sweetness and light in Ireland. There was an undercurrent which we as Aussies didn't notice and, I suppose, didn't want to notice.

Cass and I often went to Cuchulainn's Hound, one of the pubs in the village. The other was called the Minstrel Boy.

Cuchulainn's was run by a stout lady by the name of Mrs O'Connor. I never did meet Mr Dominic O'Connor. The rumour, in whispers only, was that he had taken off, to Mrs O'Connor's chagrin, not with another woman but with a man. That was a great shame then. He hadn't been seen for years. Looking at Mrs O'Connor I thought I understood why her spouse would wish to absent himself but that is another story. Like everyone else I sometimes get things wrong.

Cass and I stood at the bar drinking our pints of draft Guinness which Mrs O'Connor had just drawn from two barrels. From one she had taken the deep black silky liquid after which we both lusted and from another she had drawn the flaky, malty, foaming top that gave the glass its unique look. No other drink tastes like the draft Guinness in Ireland. She scraped the excess top from each glass with a straight-edged ruler and set them up on the counter before us. We each took a long deep gulp, swallowed and smacked our lips. Our eyes went roaming around the bar. Both sets of eyes stopped at the same place at the back of the room. There, hanging on the wall, was a magnificent set of antlers the like of which I had never seen before. As I studied them Cass began to laugh quietly. "What are you laughing at?" I asked.

"Oh, not much. I was just wondering if those antlers came from Cuchulainn's hound. The hound would look well with that head gear."

I started to laugh as well.

Now it so happened that between us and the antlers was a table at which some men were sitting. We had looked over them to study the antlers. We turned back to our drinks and were idly chatting when I heard a kind of muttering that grew louder then suddenly stopped. Looking back now I think the men thought that we were laughing at them. The room went suddenly very quiet. A large man who stood head and shoulders above Cass had left the table over which we had looked and had come to the bar. As he passed Cass he nudged him sufficiently to cause his drink to slop over the top of the glass. It was clearly a deliberate act. If the man expected a reaction he got none from Cass. I knew Cass. The man didn't. I knew how very foolishly he was acting. Looking Cass in the face he said, "Watch who you're pushing fellow."

Cass just smiled and said, "Yeah, I will. I'm getting a bit careless in my old age. Sorry mate."

That was not what this guy expected. I think that he thought Cass's reluctance to be provoked was a sign of cowardice. It was then that I noticed Mrs O'Connor reach under the bar. What it was she was reaching for I don't know because I was now fully focused on what was happening beside me. I do know that she was ahead of the game and knew her patrons. Whatever she was reaching for was quite unnecessary. Things happened very quickly then.

"I'm not your mate and you'd better be careful or you mightn't get to old age. Fellows like you should know that this is our country and we don't need any more strangers here. As far as I'm concerned strangers are bad news. They took our country from us. What we need more than interlopers like you is a united Ireland. Get it! A united Ireland! Why don't you get out and let us settle with the Germans?"

He shoved his chest against the arm in which Cass held his drink. Again some of Cass's drink slopped over the rim of his glass. I held my breath. Cass set his glass down very carefully on the bar counter, took out his handkerchief, and after wiping his hands and tunic where the Guinness had slopped, put it back in his pocket as his aggressor watched every move. Then like lightning he struck. One minute the guy was leaning forward belligerently leering at Cass, the next Cass had him by the throat up against the bar with his knee in his groin.

Cass spoke very quietly but very clearly so everyone in the bar could hear. Mrs O'Connor stood looking on with both hands still out of sight under the counter. "I don't know what I've done to upset you, mate. But if it's a fight you want then you'd better pick on someone your own size. Little fellows like me get a bit cross when we lose good Guinness because of someone's bad manners. When we catch up with Adolph, as we surely will, I'll let him know you'd like a United Ireland. I'm sure he'll listen to you just like he listened to the Poles and the French. In the meantime if it's a scrap you want with me you can have it but I warn you when you waken up in hospital you'll have things to think about other than pick fights with someone who is a guest in your country."

Cass let him go and stood waiting. The guy straightened himself up and was about to say something when Mrs. O'Connor said, "I think, Micky, you've picked on the wrong guy this time. Now go and sit down and behave like a civilised person. I don't want to be the one to have to go and tell Bridget she's a widow."

Turning to Cass she said, "I'm sorry, soldier. We're usually better behaved in this establishment. You have lost some of your drink. Here's one on the house for you and your pal," and she set up two pints on the bar in front of us. "If you need a job when this wicked war is over you have a standing offer here as my assistant barman. I could do with a real man like you in the bar - and around the house."

She gave a deep, throaty almost musical chuckle. It struck me then that maybe Mr. O'Connor didn't know the gem he had had and lost. Cass and I finished our drinks and turned to leave. It was then that Cass threw some money on the bar counter and said, "Give Micky and his mates a drink on me. Tell him I hope his dream comes true, without violent means. Sometimes when the drink's in the wit's out." And we walked out.

All that unarmed combat which Cass had under his belt had come in handy before we even got to grips with Jerry.

We told no one about that incident. But I am willing to bet my bottom dollar that if the CO had ever heard of it Cass would have been excused all drill parades for a week.

Apart from that little exception the locals treated us like visiting royalty. Some of our mates made unauthorised trips into the hinterland to look up relatives from way back. We weren't allowed to go beyond a certain limit without permission in case there was a call to arms. They went anyway; they were Aussies. None was ever caught. It was like a holiday for most of us. We didn't know what our tomorrow would bring so we set out to make the most of our today.

CHAPTER SIXTEEN

"You'll like this one, Grandson."

A sentry was posted at the camp gate. His job it was to challenge the bona fides of any person attempting entry. Life having continued as normal in spite of the war the little farm to the left inside the camp continued to supply milk to those villagers who didn't have it supplied by the milkman with his horse and cart. So a lady, her little son and daughter received an awful shock when in the dark of the evening with her milk-can in her hand she approached the gate. Suddenly, out of the darkness came a stentorian voice: "Halt! Who goes there!" The lady, scared out of her wits, exclaimed, "Jesus, Mary and Joseph! Her milk-can went flying and the children screamed."

"Holy family pass by," echoed the voice.

Somebody said on hearing that story, "With guardians like that so prepared for attack, England had no need to tremble."

"A big river ran by the end of the village street and there we found something you would find interesting, Grandson."

The swans that floated so gracefully there weren't black like ours, they were white. The only part of them that was black was their legs. The locals said that those swans would have died with pride were it not for those black legs. Cass and I were fascinated by them. We often wondered what it would be like to have a swan's egg for breakfast. We would often go down to the river bank and throw bread at them. They would come up to us and take the bread out of our hands. We were not afraid of their bites which were more like tickles than bites. Beautiful they certainly were but we were told to be careful for swans had been known to break a man's leg with their wings when they were upset.

There were many things to fill our days and keep us engaged. The army wasn't all square-bashing. Our regiment was regularly divided into two separate groups and we would go on manoeuvres. One group wore red arm-bands, they were the enemy, the other wore white, they were the good guys. We would race across the fields and through the woods firing blanks at the 'enemy', throw thunder-flashes and hurl smoke grenades. Thunder-flashes were like large squibs. You just pulled the tab and threw them at the foe's positions. They went off with a great bang. It was all a big boy's cowboys and indians. In the middle of all the serious business of learning about war some wag would shout "Bang! Bang! You're dead." It was great fun except for one poor guy. Some prankster shoved a thunder-flash under his shoulder strap and pulled the tab. There was an almighty bang and down he went. His war was over. He returned to Australia minus a lung. Thunder-flashes weren't so innocent after all.

Quite often we would organize displays of unarmed combat in the village street. The locals would gather round and "Oh!" and "Ah!" as we chucked each other about and showed how easy it was to seriously injure someone with our bare hands. The kids loved it. They would watch every move and often come and ask us to teach them how it was done.

At times we almost forgot there was a war on we were so far away from it all. I said 'almost' for we couldn't forget it completely. Most of us had a great ache. We missed Oz and the people we loved. We wanted to be into the war and get it over and done with and get home. Cass wrote to Kitty every day no matter what. His was the greatest ache of all. At night as we lay on our beds in the billet he would whisper to me that he wondered what time it was in Oz and if Kitty was in bed too. "I miss her so much, Rad," he would say. "I would gladly take on a whole bloody battalion of Jerry's alone and unarmed just to be with her. What I wouldn't give just to have her in my arms for five minutes. I hope that Raskal is taking good care of her. The sooner this bloody war is over the better I'll be pleased."

All I could say was, "It can't be much longer now, Cass. I think what is happening is that the powers-that-be want to make sure that when we go in we take Jerry by the throat and shake him till he rattles. I think they want to teach Herr Hitler a lesson that he will never forget."

I don't think it helped very much. Kitty had become his life and he missed her desperately. She seemed to be the only family he had.

CHAPTER SEVENTEEN

"One day in mid-May there was a rumour - we could hardly believe it. Next thing we knew the rumour wasn't a rumour, it was good solid hard fact. We were on our way. This time we didn't march out, we were trucked to Belfast in the late evening and were in England the next morning. Thankfully, so far as Cass was concerned, the sea was calm and he wasn't seasick. A week in England and we were on another boat, one among hundreds of boats, heading for we didn't know where. Our phoney war was over. The killing was about to begin.

It was only when we were nearly at Normandy that we were told that our destination was France. There was no doubt about it, security was the watchword of this enterprise. Our bosses had learnt their lesson from Dieppe. There was going to be no useless slaughter here because of loose tongues. On this occasion there would be no turning back. We would not stop no matter what the cost until we were in Berlin. There were not many atheists on our landing craft by the time the front end dropped on to the sands on the shore of France and we were running up the beach as if Old Nick himself was after us. He wasn't after us, he was in front of us and we had to make sure we got him before he got us.

I remember so vividly Cec Wilson's laughter when he learned we were heading for France. "I knew it," he said, "I just knew it would be France. Maybe now I'll be able to take one of those dolly birds in Paris in my arms and stab her with a bayonet that isn't made of steel. I hope she'll be gentle with me. As our preacher used to say, Heaven comes to those who believe." As usual, he threw his head back and gave one of those great, wild, reckless laughs of his. For Cec life was about today, not tomorrow.

Those were the last words I heard him speak. He had hardly set foot on French soil when he caught a bullet right between the eyes. Cec was dead before he hit the ground. But there was no time to stop to see how badly he was hit, not unless we wanted to join him on our backs on the sand as well. Those Germans were good soldiers and they, like us, were doing what they had been trained to do, kill the enemy and we were the enemy. And they had the advantage. We were running across open ground. They were lying well above us on their stomachs letting rip with all they had. How we ever got up that beach I don't know. I do know that I stuck close to Corporal Carrington, who seemed to have a charmed life. He would run pell-mell until he was out of breath then drop onto the sand. When he had his breath back he would leap up and take off again. I ran a few paces behind him. We got to the base of the cliffs. There we lay and studied the higher ground. We could see clearly some Germans using a mortar with deadly effect. They were blasting their way along the beach as if they were on a training exercise. God knows how many of our mates they killed. Cass didn't study too long. He got up on his hands and knees, unhooked a hand grenade from his belt and ran almost bent double to just below where the mortar crew was. Then lying back down on the sand he pulled the pin from the grenade, held it in his hand whilst I counted one, two, three. I thought, 'My God, if he doesn't throw the bloody thing it will blow both his hands off,' then he threw it backwards over his head. His aim was deadly. It exploded not on the ground as was the usual case but in the air just above the mortar. The result was a massacre. There was no more mortar fire after that.

What he had done was hold the grenade to the point where it had only two seconds to go before it exploded. He knew his explosives alright. When he threw it it exploded in the air in a kind of inverted V just above the mortar crew. They had no chance. If it had hit the ground before exploding because the explosion goes up in a kind of V there was a chance that some of the mortar crew would have survived and might have hurled a grenade back where he lay. Cass was way ahead of that. He was a one man killing-machine. Next minute he was up and climbing the cliff. This war would be over pretty damn soon if he had anything to do with it.

"But I don't mean to dwell on the war too much, Ben. I tell you this only to show you what kind of man Cass was."

CHAPTER EIGHTEEN

Well, we had established our bridgehead and the war rolled on. Soon we were in Paris where I couldn't help thinking of Cec and our other mates who didn't make it. Cass received his letters from Kitty and still he wrote to her every day except on those days when he was too busy sending little lead messengers to those German guys who were as keen to kill us as we were to kill them. War is such a senseless thing. There we were doing our best to kill as many people as we could when in happier times we might have been having a beer with them, slapping them on the back and calling them good mates.

All that summer we fought our way across Europe. The things that Cass did were beyond belief. How he survived I'll never know. When I thought afterwards of some of the things he did I realised just what a fine soldier he was. All his risks were calculated ones. Well has it been said since that He Who Dares Wins. Cass dared all the time and kept winning. Many a time I prayed that he had calculated correctly when I saw him rush in where no angel would have dared to tread. Always he came out smiling. By the beginning of 1945 he had collected two awards for gallantry and was wearing a sergeant's stripes. He was offered a commission in the field but refused on the basis that he wanted to be in there with his mates. "I'm not a team man. I'm better doing my own thing. And anyway I'm no good at paper-work," he said. I was glad that he refused that commission because I felt that with him ahead of me I was safe.

"This is the bit that all this has been leading up to, Grandson. This is the bit where I want to hear what you would have done."

One day when there was a lull in the fighting the mail came and Cass received a bundle of letters. It had been some time since our mail had caught up with us. He went off to a quiet spot as he usually did to read them. When he came back he wasn't smiling as he usually was after he had read them. His face was deathly pale. I knew immediately there was something wrong.

"I needn't remind you that it was going on for two years since Cass had last seen Kitty."

"Bad news, Cass?" I asked.

"Yeah, it's bad news alright, Rad. Raskal's dead."

He told me. Kitty had taken Raskal to the local park and had flung the ball for him all morning. They were returning home along the footpath beside the tennis court when a tennis ball came over the fence, plopped to the ground a few centimetres from Raskal's nose and bounced into the road. Raskal not being on a leash jumped after it right into the path of an oncoming car. He caught the ball alright but the car caught him. The passenger-side mudguard knocked him forward directly in line with the front wheel. Raskal had no chance. The lady driving the car stopped immediately. She was almost as traumatised as Kitty. The screams of both of them brought the people from the tennis club running to the scene. The police arrived and Kitty was taken home. What was left of Raskal was gathered up and taken to the garden of the house where he had lived with Kitty. There a caring police officer dug a hole and buried him. He even placed a little cross at the end of the grave. For days afterwards Kitty was inconsolable. Her one true four-legged friend was gone. The lady driver of the car, after she had recovered, would sometimes go to visit her but it didn't help very much. Kitty didn't make friends easily and she wanted Raskal back. She didn't want sympathy. More than anything else she wanted Cass but he was far far away.

62

In her letter then and the ones that followed the depth of her grief was evident. She told Cass how much she missed Raskal. At night he would sleep beside her bed. In those nights when she couldn't sleep and would lie thinking of Cass she would often put her hand down and stroke Raskal. She often went to sleep with him licking her hand. Now she was completely alone. She didn't know what to do. In the end she could stand it no longer. The loneliness was driving her mad. One day she packed up her few belongings and returned to Melbourne; to my Mum and Dad who had often invited her to come and stay with them now that Elsie and Bob had gone to live in another suburb nearer Bob's work.

CHAPTER NINETEEN

That was only meant to be a temporary thing and she did not want to impose. Even though my Mum and Dad begged her to stay she felt that she was being a misery-guts and was spreading her misery around her so she found a little apartment and went to live on her own. One day Elsie went to see her and said that it wasn't sensible for her to stay fretting on her own. The war would end soon and Cass would be home and all would be well. Kitty's reply was that that it seemed that this bloody war would never end and she would never see Cass again. It seemed that the spirit had gone out of her. She was back being that little brown mouse again. Only this time she was miserable beyond words. She didn't seem to be able to do anything to help herself. Mum and Elsie discussed it and decided that what she needed was a job. They went through the newspapers together and found an ad. which sought someone to assist in a little corner deli. Training would be given. Elsie talked Kitty into going for an interview. The shopkeeper was a man in his thirties. He asked Kitty several questions and when he heard her husband was a soldier out fighting somewhere in Europe he asked no more questions.

"The job is yours, Miss, if you want it. You can start tomorrow from nine to six Monday to Saturday with a half day off on Wednesday. If you don't like it all you have to do is say so and there will be no hard feelings. Would you like to have a go?"

Kitty started work the next day. Mum and Elsie's ploy had worked. Kitty got a new direction in life. The change in her letters was noticeable immediately. The depression was lifting. Cass breathed a sigh of relief. It seemed that all was well. Once more he could apply himself to soldiering .There were times when I was sure he thought he could win the war all on his own. The solid fact was he missed his wife like he had never missed anyone and wanted to be with her and hold her in his arms. He never could stop talking about her.

We had been away from Australia for nearly two years. It wasn't only Kitty who thought it was a long two years. Cass and I had had enough of the killing and longed to be back in Oz once again. I promised him that the day we arrived back I would take him and Kitty and the whole family to Young and Jackson's pub in Flinders Street. I would lock all the doors and we could all drink until the police came and arrested us.

He laughed at that and said, "We could even invite the cops in for a drink, Rad, and if they refused we could fight them. It would, I think, be less dangerous than fighting Jerry."

"You can fight the cops on your own, Cass. All I want is a barrel full of VB."

And so we laughed and so we fought on. The nearer we got to Germany the harder the Germans fought. I think most of us prayed that if we were to catch a bullet it would be quick and final. None of us wanted to be blinded or maimed or made lesser men.

Each time the mail came, it didn't come every day, Cass would take his letters, as usual, and go off to read them in private. Usually he came back smiling. Kitty was enjoying her work. She was saving money to buy furniture for the house they would have when Cass got back home. At times she said she was a bit down but she was getting there. Maybe when he got home Cass would find her another dog but she would wait until then because he was good at picking dogs, she said.

CHAPTER TWENTY

I remember well the day the letter came that changed things so irrevocably in Cass's world, and mine too. It was one of several that Cass took off to read in a quiet place. It was some time before he returned. When he did he was white and trembling. When I looked at him I knew something was badly wrong. The thought went through my mind that something terrible had happened to Kitty. Something terrible had happened, but not in the manner I had thought. Without saying a word he did what he had never done before and handed me one of Kitty's letters to read. The ink was streaked and blotched with tear stains. It really was a mess. I wasn't sure if I should read it or not as I didn't want to trespass into his private life. But it was quite clear that that was what he wanted so I took it and read it. If I had been smashed in the guts by a rifle butt I could not have felt more winded. No wonder he was white and trembling. I think I was almost as hurt as he was. But no, I couldn't be. Nobody else could have felt the pain of that letter like Cass. It was a catastrophe. I didn't know it then but it was a death sentence. His Kitty had betrayed him. I couldn't believe it. I had to read it twice just to be sure that I had it right.

My dear Cass,
    This is the most terrible letter I have ever had to write but I must write it because if I don't tell you someone else will and I want you to know from me where the blames lies. It lies with me. I have told you how since Raskal was killed I have felt so alone. You were so far

away and I missed so much having your arms around me and being kissed and pampered by you like I had never been in my whole life before I met you. It was you, Cass, who really showed me what life could be like. You transported me, took me above the clouds. Made me feel that I was a somebody who meant something to somebody. Then you were gone. I thought getting a job would help and it did, to some extent, but I missed you more and more with the passage of each day. It seems like a lifetime since you kissed me goodbye. Ricky, he's Eric Dickson who owns the shop, has been very good to me. He pretended not to notice when he would sometimes find me crying in the storeroom. Then one day an old gentleman who came to the shop regularly with his wife came in alone. I asked him where his wife was. He told me that she was at home and that she didn't want to accompany him to the shop because they had had some very bad news. They had just been advised by the War Office that their son who was a soldier somewhere in Europe had been killed and she was taking it so very badly she couldn't stop crying. Then he began to cry too. He said that he and his wife had looked forward so much to the day when their son would come back. Now he would never return. That set me going. I thought of you and thought that maybe you would never come back. It was all too much. Rick tried to comfort both of us. I managed to stop crying and Ricky took the old man home. That, Cass, was one of the worst days of my life. After they had gone I went into the storeroom sat down on a carton in there and howled. That's where Ricky found me when he came back. I just couldn't stop sobbing. He tried to talk sense into me, said that the war couldn't go on for much longer and that you would soon be home. It made no difference. I was just broken-hearted. I had bottled it up for so long that I just fell apart. It was then that Ricky put his arms around me, pulled me up close against him and hugged me. We stood there like that for I don't know how long he with his arms around me and me with my head on his shoulder. Then the shop door bell rang and he pulled away to attend a customer who had just entered. After the customer was gone he came back to me. I was still in the storeroom. He asked me if I was feeling better. I couldn't speak. I just nodded. Then he took me in his arms again and this time he kissed me, first on the cheek and then on the lips. He said not to worry, that he would look after me till you came home again; that all would be well; that I was just lonely and had allowed things to get on top of me. That, Cass, was the start of it. I didn't really want his arms around me. I wanted yours but you weren't there and I needed somebody. From then on it progressed until every time I went into the storeroom he would follow me, put his arms round me and fondle me. One evening he walked me home from the shop. I invited him in for a cup of tea and he ended up staying the night. Now I spend every night with him. It's not that I love him, Cass, I don't. I love you but I just couldn't stand the lonely nights. You weren't there and I didn't even have Raskal. It isn't his fault, he's a good man. It's my fault. I think I might have led him on. You see, I needed to be loved. Now I feel like a wanton woman. I know I have betrayed you. But put yourself in my position. I didn't want to let

68

you down but the loneliness was driving me mad. I'm sorry, Cass, and if you never want to see me again I'll understand. But I still love you. I'll always love you. What am I to do? Oh, what am I to do! I want nothing more than to be in your arms again and have you inside me. That's when I am in that heaven to which you introduced me. I only ever wanted you but then you weren't there and I didn't know if you would ever come back. I still don't know and I want you, need you so much. I want you back so much. That's what I truly want. Cass, no matter what I will always be your loving wife. Please say you forgive me. I'll always love you.

Kitty xxxxx

CHAPTER TWENTY ONE

"Now, Grandson, what does one say about a letter like that to a man who had lived only for the day when he could return to that wife and take her in his arms. She herself had said it; it was betrayal like no other. I didn't know what to say. I felt for Kitty and could understand her loneliness but at the same time thought that other wives had had to put up with the loneliness so why couldn't she? She could have done better. She had knocked the stuffing out of my mate and I hated her for it. What was I to say to him? I couldn't tell him to cut the cable and let her go. To have said that would have been reckless in the extreme. I had to try to retrieve the situation."

"Cass," I said, "you have to do as she says and put yourself in her position. She's just really a slip of a girl who was on her own and taking your separation badly. She was a plum ripe for the picking. Kitty had been loved by you like she had never been loved before. She had had a man's arms around her and a man's loving. She had never experienced anything like that before she met you. It was so good she got to like it; to need it. Those seventy two days of being loved by you every night had taken her into a world that was like heaven. Suddenly you were gone and she was bereft. As you know nature hates a vacuum and she was in a vacuum. You'll never know how much she loved you. When she was at her lowest ebb along comes an opportunist who should have known better. All he had to do was give her a little comfort, tell her he would look after her till you came home and, poor girl, she was lost. I have no doubt he groomed her, Cass. Turned the poor girl's head to the point where she didn't know where she was. This is your problem, Cass, and you are man enough to sort it out for yourself. Write back today and tell her you understand. Tell her you forgive her. Tell her to ditch Ricky immediately and leave the shop and all will be forgiven. Tell her that the war will soon be over; that you will be home soon and she will be loved more than ever before. Tell her that you will always love her."

I wasn't surprised when he took my advice. You see I knew my man and I knew how much he loved Kitty and what she meant to him. He wrote to her that day. For once he told me what he put in the letter.

I thought that maybe he had gone too far but it was his call and who was I to tell him how to run his life. I had given him what I thought was good advice. Advice that poured oil on troubled waters and I hoped and prayed would save the marriage, sort things out and also save his sanity. Cass was my mate and all I wanted to do was to give him a little comfort in his hour of need.

In his letter he said he understood and that he forgave her. He said that it wasn't her fault. Loneliness was a terrible illness. Ricky should have known better and left another man's wife alone. That as far as he was concerned that scumbag was nothing more than an opportunist who had taken advantage of a lonely little girl when she was at her lowest ebb and that if he didn't leave her alone immediately the moment his feet touched Australian soil the first thing he would do would be to kill the mongrel. If he didn't kill the sod he would cut his balls off. By the time he was finished with him no other young and lonely wife would be sucked into betrayal by him. And why the hell wasn't the coward out fighting for his country instead of sitting back letting another man do his fighting for him while he shafted that man's wife? 'I promise you, Kitty, if he doesn't leave you alone immediately the first thing I'll do will be to kill the mongrel as soon as I get back. You know me, Kitty, my love, I don't break my promises. I've killed so many innocents in my life, men who have personally done me no harm, that killing a guilty sod like him will make little difference one way or the other.'

I waited with trepidation for the reply to that letter. Sometimes I thought Kitty wouldn't reply. I thought wrongly. She did reply and I almost wished she hadn't. Whilst we waited I noticed the change in Cass. From being deliberate and calculating in the risks he took it seemed to me that he had thrown caution to the winds and no longer cared about his safety. It was as if a great hate had settled upon him. He had become jumpy and ill at ease. More inward looking and withdrawn. There were times when he even snapped at me. No man wanted the war to end more quickly than he.

CHAPTER TWENTY TWO

When Kitty's reply came it surprised me. I thought she would leap at the forgiveness offered. She didn't. She said that she had told Ricky that she must give him up immediately or Cass would kill him. Ricky had said that he didn't think that was likely to happen. Australia was a civilised country and Cass was a civilised man. Cass would not kill him. It was alright for him to kill Germans, they were the enemy and the free world had to defend itself against such tyrants. It wasn't alright for him to kill fellow Australians. Cass knew as well as he did that the bible said 'Thou shalt not kill'. He begged her to stay with him saying that he would talk to Cass when the war was over and he came home. He'd explain that all he had done was keep a sad and lonely little girl happy while her husband was far away fighting. He was sure that when they met he and Cass could be friends. They could work something out. He asked her to tell Cass that the reason why he wasn't in uniform, much though he wanted to be, was because he had an irregular heart-beat and had been rejected as unfit for army service.

That letter just about drove Cass insane. "The slimy scumbag," he said. "Sweet-talking Kitty into believing that. Him quoting the bible to me with his 'Thou shalt not'. There are a lot of Thou Shalt Nots in the bible. Thou shalt not commit adultery, Thou shalt not covet another man's wife. If he doesn't leave her I will kill him with my bare hands when I get back."

That was the start of a flow of letters all going to show that Cass would forgive Kitty if she left Ricky and her replies saying she didn't know what to do about Ricky. She didn't know how to give him up because he had been so good to her. Talk about a Mexican stand-off. This was a Mexican stand-off and how.

And as the letters chased each other backwards and forwards across Europe we chased the enemy back towards Germany. The change in Cass became ever more noticeable. They say that anger is a short form of madness and I have no doubt there is a lot of truth in that. Cass then was always angry and thus he was always mad. Some of the things he did made me wonder if he didn't care if the war ended quickly any more, he just wanted to die. For sure, he had the death-wish. All that he had been living for for the past two years had been taken from him. Life meant nothing to him anymore.

In the middle of this toing and froing of the letters we edged slowly forward. The Germans were good fighters. They were our enemies but I must say they fought heroically. We weren't fighting the Nazis, we were fighting ordinary, I could say, extraordinary, decent Germans citizens who played the game by the rules. That is not to say that both sides didn't break the rules. In the heat of battle rules do get broken because if they aren't you die and I, for one, did not want to die. In the middle of a great rush forward you don't take prisoners, you kill.

CHAPTER TWENTY THREE

I well remember the day Cass won his VC. I won't tell you all of the gory details. This story is not about his heroism, which is legendary. This story is about another side of my best mate and you should see both sides.

"If you want to know how he won the Victoria Cross you, being a top gun young lawyer, Grandson, will have no difficulty finding the citation that told the world that Australia was not lacking when it came to defending liberty and the right to freedom. I will say only this, it was a brutal episode."

Good men on both sides became the cannon fodder that left some widows to mourn for the remainder of their lives. It left Danny Simmons with a leg missing and George Sanders in a dark world for the rest of his life. A blast of shrapnel from an exploding shell left Sandy with a face that wasn't a face anymore. I don't think he would have minded that so much if he could have kept his eyes. Maybe it was a good thing he couldn't see the disfigurement.

We had charged forward to do the impossible. It was a suicide run. All round me my mates were falling. But we had been told to go and go we must. I got a wallop on the head from what I know not and went down. That fall may have saved my life. I wasn't knocked out, just dazed. I fell forward on my face. When I raised my head I saw Cass racing forward. A machine-gun was chattering, grenades were bursting all around. The air was a choir of singing bullets as they passed over my head. Every moment I expected to see him go down. I looked on with shame, horror, admiration and pride. He was doing what none of the rest of us could do, he was giving it back to Jerry. He was a human tornado sweeping all before him. I was ashamed because I was lying there and couldn't get up. What I was seeing held me in thrall. At the same time I was ashamed because I wasn't there beside him as I had always been in the past. I was in horror for him for I expected every moment to be his last. Cass at that moment was a man possessed and to be admired above all. All I could do was lie there and share in his glory. He was an Aussie and I was proud.

I don't know how long I lay there. I might have passed out. Suddenly I was alert to the fact that everything had gone very quiet. Next moment Cass was beside me saying, "Come on, Rad. Why are you lying there having a siesta in the middle of all the fun. Come and give me a hand with Danny and Sandy." It was as if he was in the middle of a training exercise. I reached up my hand and he pulled me up. When I had steadied myself we both went to where Danny was lying, calling out, "Somebody help me! Somebody help! Oh, God, somebody help me!" A few metres from him George Sanders was on his feet staggering in circles howling. "I can't see! I can't see!"

"It was on that day, Ben, that I realized there is no romance in war."

"You get Sandy," Cass said. "I'll handle Danny."

He bent down over Danny and said, "It's okay, Fanny, I mean Danny", and he laughed, "I've got you. Give me your hand, mate."

Danny raised his hand, Cass took it, bent down and lifted Danny across his shoulders in a fireman's lift and began to walk back to where the ambulance was waiting. I followed, holding Sandy's elbow. I tried not to look at his face. The sight of it will stay with me forever. Our lieutenant met us half way. He helped place Danny and Sandy both in the same ambulance. When he had done that he turned to Cass, threw his arms round him and said, "Bloody hell, Cass," (I noticed he didn't call him Sergeant) "I've never seen anything like it. You've done what the whole bloody lot of us put together couldn't do. You are surely the bravest man I have ever known. You make me proud to be an Aussie. You'll get the Victoria Cross for this if I have anything to do with it."

Cass stood looking at the ground. He shuffled his feet in that peculiar way of his before he spoke. "Well, I couldn't keep on letting them kill my mates, sir, could I?"

"I suppose you couldn't," said the lieutenant.

It was only then that I noticed the Luger pistol sticking in his belt.

"Where the hell did you get that, Cass?" I asked.

"Some German officer tried to kill me with it. He wasn't fast enough. You know, Rad, in this madness it's dog eat dog. I got in first. I'm sorry I had to kill him. He was a brave man. I took this to remember him by. Never know when it might come in handy. I'm taking it back to Oz. It's the only trophy I'll take back."

I'm sure that at that moment Cass knew what he was going to do with that Luger back in Oz. I think that I knew then too. I hoped I was wrong.

There were many more skirmishes after that. And always he was in the forefront, reckless. I was so concerned for him that I went to our lieutenant and told him that I thought Cass had done enough. "It's time he was given a rest," I said. "His good luck can't last for ever."

"What are you, Corporal?" asked the officer. "His nursemaid? Sergeant Carrington is a soldier. Am I to stand down every soldier who might get killed fighting the enemy? Soldiers get killed in war. When he, himself, comes to me and asks to be stood down I will listen. Until then, Corporal, I suggest you leave him to work his own salvation. I wish I had a hundred like him. We could win this bloody war on our own if I had." I was rebuffed and that was that. That officer was one officer I did not love.

Suddenly we were in Berlin. Adolph had done to himself what the German Valkyrie mob had failed to do. He was gone and the war in Europe was over. It was time to get back to Oz. I could hardly believe that Cass and I had made it through without a scratch. And that was when our paths separated for a little while.

CHAPTER TWENTY FOUR

Cass didn't come back to Oz directly. He was side-tracked to Buckingham Palace where the Queen's father pinned the VC on his chest.

"Did you know, Grandson, that only one hundred Australians have been awarded that little piece of metal, in the form of a cross which bears the words, For Valour. I think it is the highest award given anywhere for gallantry. It is not given lightly. No woman has ever been awarded it probably because they never had the opportunity. But, given time that will come too."

At the presentation ceremony Cass was shuffling his feet and trying not to look down as he usually did but to look his King in the face. I think to make Cass feel more at ease, as the King pinned the medal to his chest he said, in his so carefully measured halting speech, for he had a massive stammer to overcome, "I'm almost as nervous as you, Sergeant. I'll try not to prick you with the pin," and he smiled. The ice was broken. Cass stopped shuffling and said "I hope not, Sir, I just can't stand the sight of blood." They both laughed.

Cass had a treat in store. I knew that he was dreading that long sea- journey home. He just hated the thought of being cooped up in a cabin being sea-sick all day. Somebody must have known about his malady for he was flown home. Yes, flown all the way back home to Australia in those days when flying was reserved only for the privileged and he was treated like royalty. His kit-bag was carried on to the plane for him; he wasn't searched. Everybody wanted to shake his hand. This was one of the few brave men who had gone above and beyond for the land they loved. And then he was at Melbourne airport. The news had travelled ahead of him. The airport was crowded. The press were there in droves. The Governor of Victoria was there with an entourage every member of which thought they were privileged to be on the brink of the first to meet Sergeant Carrington, VC in Australia.

"I regret to say it, Ben, but they were all disappointed. With the help of a baggage handler his kit-bag was off the plane first and he was in a taxi heading into the city, alone. I can tell you that caused consternation at the airport. Nobody knew what to do. The Governor's lackeys ran about in panic trying to locate him. The press minions were frustrated. They had just missed their great photo shoot. Little did they know then that they had a far more sought after series of photos ahead of them."

"Cass was doing simply what he said he would do. He had said that the first thing he would do when he arrived on Australian soil would be to seek out Mr Eric Dickson and kill him. Cass always kept his word."

CHAPTER TWENTY FIVE

"Would you like a cup of tea, Grandson?" asked my grandpa.

I didn't want a cup of tea, I was so engrossed in the story but I knew Grandpa did so I put the kettle on.

Grandpa smacked his lips. "Can't beat a good cup of tea," he said. "Now to get on with the story."

The taxi drew up in front of the shop. Cass paid off the driver, hauled out his kit-bag and waited until the taxi had taken off. Only then did he place his kit-bag against the wall at the end of the shop window, open it, make two withdrawals and close it again. He left it leaning against the wall. He opened the shop door and walked in. The door-bell rang as he entered. The man bending over some papers on the shop counter looked up. He saw before him a man in army dress uniform with three stripes on each sleeve, a bundle of letters in one hand and a Luger in the other. He knew trouble when he saw it. He didn't have to ask who this man was. He swallowed twice then in a half-strangled voice called out, "Kitty! Kitty!" Kitty came running from the storeroom behind him. She took one look at her husband and shouted, "Cass! Oh, Cass, at last you've come home!" Cass ignored her.

Addressing the man behind the counter he said in a very quiet voice, "So you are the Eric Dickhead who worms his way into the knickers of another man's wife."

"You must be Cass? Hang on a minute. Don't do anything we'll all regret. Let's talk," said Dickson, for that was the man. "And the name is DickSON, not Dickhead."

"Maybe I made a mistake. Maybe it's Prickson? Son of the

Prick would suit you better. I said I would come and I said I would kill you if you didn't leave my wife alone. Well here I am."

It was Kitty who spoke. She was frightened, very frightened. Not for herself because she believed, and rightly so, that Cass would never harm her. She feared for Ricky. He had been there and given her comfort and satisfied her biological needs when Cass was far away. It may seem strange but I think she loved both men who were now facing each other. I have no doubt that she loved Cass more but he wasn't there when she needed him. In some naïve, unworldly way I think she thought that when he came home they could talk it over very civilly. You see, Grandson, Kitty had no experience of life and she had lost sight of reality. Hers was a very small world with only a handful of people in it. She was in the middle of a situation that even the most worldly would have found difficult to manage. The most worldly would have been more cunning; would not have left themselves so exposed to hurt. At that moment I am sure that she knew something terrible was going to happen and she must do her best to prevent it. The simple fact was that there was nothing she could do. Their fate was already written in the stars. She had betrayed the man who loved her, whose life she was. She stood there, her face drained of blood, shaking violently. In great distress she said, "Oh, please, Cass, please. Listen to me. It wasn't Ricky's fault, it was mine. I missed you so much and I was so lonely. All Ricky did was carry me over the bad patch. Please let us talk. Please, Cass."

"Sure he carried you over the bad patch and got into your knickers at the same time. Lots of wives were lonely when their husbands were far away. I was lonely too. Every day I longed to take you in my arms and love you and be loved by you but you were in someone else's arms. I don't blame you, Kitty. I know what loneliness is like. I don't blame you at all." Pointing at Dickson, he said, "I blame him. That mongrel there. The time for talking is over."

Turning to Dickson directly again he said, "All the time she was writing those letters to me and crying her heart out you were working on her for no other reason than that you knew she was vulnerable. All you wanted was to get inside her and gratify your lust. No, I don't blame Kitty. I will never blame her. I will always love her. I blame you. Well, there are the letters which you should have read. They will show you how much she loved me, you mongrel," and he hurled the bundle of letters at Dickson. "But you will never read them for today, one way or the other, you are going to meet your Maker. Maybe He will forgive you. I never will. But don't let it be said I didn't give you a chance." Turning the Luger with its butt towards Dickson he placed it on the counter between them.

Dickson ignored the pistol. Standing looking fearfully at Cass with his hands at chest level the palms outwards he said, "before you do anything we'll both regret I think you should hear my side."

"You haven't got a side," cut in Cass. "And you sure as hell aren't going to sweet-talk me like you sweet-talked Kitty into saying that all is forgiven by saying that all's fair in love and war. Some things just aren't fair."

"I'm not trying to sweet-talk you. I just want you to know that I'm not a coward. I'm not a coward. I applied to join the army three times and was rejected three times. They wouldn't even take me as an ambulance man. They said I was too big a risk. I wondered what I could do to help the war-effort. That's why I employed Kitty. I thought that giving a fighting man's wife a job would be helping at least one of our soldiers. I didn't know what I was letting myself in for. You see Kitty is a young woman. I can tell you now she missed you terribly. Her main subject of conversation when she first came to the shop was you. She needed comforting, loving - a lot of loving. I could see that."

The words were tumbling out of Dickson. He was stammering and stuttering, almost gabbling. He knew that he was in deep trouble and only his tongue could save him. He should have kept his mouth shut and taken full responsibility and left it there for the more he talked the deeper the hole he dug.

"And you didn't miss your chance. You, sure as hell, gave her the loving."

Dickson ignored the interruption and continued. "No, it wasn't like that. Not like that at all. Things were fine at first," he continued. "Then she began coming to work with low-cut blouses. She would bend down in front of me so that I couldn't help seeing that she had no bra. She would brush against me behind the counter as she passed or she would squeeze close to me as she went through the door into the storeroom. Often she would rub against me to pick something from a shelf. In the storeroom she would climb the stepladder to reach something from a higher shelf so that I couldn't help looking up her skirt. Her perfume nearly drove me mad. And she was always posing, posturing and bending down sticking out her butt in front of me."

Kitty interrupted. "It wasn't like that, Cass. It wasn't. I swear it wasn't."

Dickson ignored her and continued.

"Kitty has a beautiful figure. And she knew how to flaunt it. It was quite obvious what she wanted. She was a plum ripe for the picking. If I hadn't picked her somebody else would have. That day in the storeroom when I found her crying was only one of many when I found her there. On that day I let my guard down. I think she set me up. I'm a man, Cass. I admit it. I'm human. There's only so much a man can take. I shouldn't have done it. I wonder what you would have done in my position? And as for getting into her knickers, I never did. She didn't wear any."

"You rat. You dirty rat. It's not enough that you shaft my wife but you blame her for it. You've said your say now listen to me. Nothing you could say would stop me loving my wife. I'll always love her and I will always forgive her but I will not forgive you."

Pushing the gun towards Dickson he said, "Take that. Go into that storeroom where it all began and do the right thing, for if you don't I'll do it for you. Prove that in spite of your irregular heart-beat and your inability to go to war you are still a man. I will tell the police that when you saw me you were so overcome with shame that you just couldn't be stopped. That way you might retain some respect though I doubt it. I might even attend your funeral."

CHAPTER TWENTY SIX

"Thinking the whole thing through over the years since, Grandson, I believe that Dickson was a poor wretch more to be pitied than blamed. There may even be more than a grain of truth in what he said. Cass was too blinded by his betrayal to think straight. There he was in that shop hearing at first-hand what he didn't want to hear or believe. Not only had his wife betrayed him but she was being described as just a common little tart. That was too much for him."

"You're a man, Ben, you know what men are like. Where the twos and threes are gathered together the talk if it doesn't begin with sex gets around to it eventually. I don't know about the girls but I'm sure it's the same with them. Girls have their feelings too. We all think about it. Don't be in any doubt about that. Anyone who tells you they don't think about sex just isn't trustworthy. Don't believe them. Presidents, princes, priests, paupers and peasants don't go through life without thinking about it. That prim and proper sweet old lady who goes to church every Sunday and sings in the choir thinks and fantasises about it. I'm willing to be bet that even that old bachelor in Rome has given it more than a passing thought. If he doesn't now he sure as hell did when he was a young man, though I wouldn't embarrass him by asking. His errant priests have thought enough about it to put him in the picture. Poor man. Herr Freud sitting reflecting in Vienna knew what he was talking about. Sex is what makes the world go round and sometimes for some of us brings the world crashing about our ears. It lost an English king his crown; it had an American president impeached; it cost Oscar Wilde, genius though he thought he was, his reputation, liberty and, indirectly, his life, so what chance had Ricky Dickson trapped in his little corner store all day and every day with a virile, nubile young woman the proximity of whom was driving him mad?"

"But back to the story. Dickson pushed the weapon away. Cass pushed it back. A struggle took place between them in the course of which Cass wrapped his arms around Dickson and pulled him bodily over the counter."

"You will remember, Grandson, that Cass was an expert in unarmed combat. I will admit that he took advantage of his expertise. But in fairness to him he had been betrayed and I would say was not thinking straight. In the wrestling match that followed Dickson had no chance. Who came into possession of the Luger was never quite clear. The two men fell to the floor where they continued to struggle. Kitty stood agape paralysed with fright. She heard the explosion when the gun went off. She saw Cass sitting on the floor with the gun in his hand. She saw Dickson lying with blood pouring from his stomach. Screaming she ran through the front door into the street."

Two men carrying furniture from a removalist's van further up the street heard the screaming and saw her run. They dropped the sofa they were carrying and ran towards her. The first man put his arms around her and said, "It's alright darl. It's alright. You're safe now. I've got you".

Kitty was hysterical. She kept repeating, "He's killed him! He's killed him. He said he would. He said he would. Now he's done it. Oh, God! Oh my God! What have I done!"

A posse of police arrived led by detective inspector Robert Burns McKye.

'Robbie', as he was known to all his friends, had been sitting in his office listening to the radio commentary on the imminent arrival at Melbourne airport of the last Australian VC of the war. The commentator had reached the point where he was telling his listeners how the aircraft had landed but there was no sign of the VC and the Governor and his entourage were somewhat nonplussed. Where was the hero? That was the sixty four thousand dollar question. It was then that Robbie's listening was interrupted by his call out to an emergency that required his presence with the utmost urgency.

CHAPTER TWENTY SEVEN

Robbie was the product of a Glaswegian father and a Yorkshire mother. He first saw the light of day in a dank, damp, dark, dismal cell-like dump that passed for living accommodation in a tenement, a large concrete pile where the sun never shone, that smelt of urine, faeces and other things foul in the area of Glasgow known as the Gallowgate. The people who lived there hated their lives. They were trapped with no hope of escape. The men drank their dole money, came home from the pub, vomited and beat their wives. The wives sometimes wore dark glasses, if they had them, and excused their black eyes and bruised faces to their friends by telling how they had opened the wardrobe door awkwardly or tripped on the linoleum and caught their face on the corner of a table as they fell. Not once would they blame their husbands for to tell was to be a snitch and they were not snitches.

Those wives knew their place. That place was to serve their husband, to comfort him, bear his children, make his meals, scrub, clean, launder and keep a home. Their husband was lord and master. What were they but slaves? If their husbands beat them they must be doing something wrong. Domestic violence was something that didn't exist. Go to the police because they had a black eye or bruised face? Don't be daft! Wasn't the police force comprised of men? What would those men do? They would tell them to get the hell out of it and go home and respect their husbands. Their husbands were entitled to beat their wives. Hadn't a good Scottish court said that a man was permitted to beat his wife provided he used a stick no thicker than his thumb? It was a man's world. Yes, it was a good world, for the men.

In those tenements was a world of hard men and pathetic women. The female friends of the women who were beaten sympathised and made the same excuses when it was their turn. Their daughters had their curiosity about sex whetted when they found themselves pregnant and had to marry in haste if they knew the father and he hadn't done a runner. For them, the vicious cycle continued. The young men who couldn't find work, or didn't want it, joined street gangs and took over the streets.

"You may think, Grandson, that the reputed African gangs that are said to be causing problems in the streets of Melbourne are bad but they are not a patch on the Glasgow gangs of that time. Those gangs delighted in arming themselves with large potatoes with a razor blade stuck in the middle of them. With those they would surround any unaccompanied person they found in the street. 'Can your mother sew?' they would ask. No matter what the answer if the victim didn't run and run fast they would slash him in the face and say, 'Well, tell her to sew that.' I say 'him' because it was usually young or vulnerable males that they slashed. Never females. Females were not slashed out of some peculiar or contorted form of chivalry. Those were bitter twisted young men, the product of their environment and they got away with it for a long time. Then there came one chief constable who took them on, rallied his troops and smashed their gangs. That police officer, long gone, is to be commended for in a small but significant way he set the future of Glasgow in a different direction. Glasgow is now one of the premier cities in the United Kingdom."

"McKye senior was one of the exceptions to the general rule and there were exceptions. He didn't drink or smoke but he thought a lot. His wife thought a lot too. Both of them could see the writing on the wall for their son. They wanted their boy to have a long and happy life. He would achieve neither happiness nor longevity in Glasgow. At that time, Grandson, Glasgow had the unenviable distinction of having the shortest- lived citizens in the whole of Great Britain. I suppose, looking at it as a cynic would, that was not a bad thing, for there were fewer cases of dementia and Alzheimers." Grandpa chuckled ruefully then.

One night just after dark, he and Mrs McKye with such of their worldly goods as they could manage in two large suitcases and their young son walking beside them caught a bus outside the tenement. They went to the docks and boarded a ship for Oz.

During the several weeks they spent on that ship the McKyes enjoyed life as they had never enjoyed it before. It was like a holiday in a first class hotel. They had more food than they could eat. Never before had they seen so much food. There was a library with a good range of books. Sometimes there were concerts in which the passengers were invited to take part. It was bliss. And as the ship neared Australia and sailed into the sunshine Robbie's parents thanked their God for 'Geeing them the guid sense that would gee them and their bairn a bonny life.' It was as if the crew were all slaves with no other object in mind than to attend to their every want. The boy ran around the deck and played with other children. The waiters in the dining-room loved him and made him feel like a grown-up when they allowed him to help collect the empty dishes from the table. They gave him extra helpings of custard and jelly. Already he was in his heaven.

His parents had sense enough to appreciate that it couldn't last and they didn't want it to. They wanted to be in Oz and start their new life with their beloved Robbie. One morning early when the sun was already climbing the bright blue sky the ship docked in Melbourne. The McKyes, father, mother and son, said their goodbyes to the crew, picked up their suitcases and walked down the gangway to a new life.

They all loved their adopted country from the moment they sat foot in it. Robbie grew into a fine man. From the age of ten his one ambition was to join the police. His parents encouraged him. They wanted their son on the right side of the law right from the beginning. By the time he was thirty Robbie was a detective inspector. That was something of a feat in those days but he was the best they had and he couldn't be denied. He was to stay in the rank for several years for he had to wait to fill dead men's shoes. Police officers went to pension after twenty five years service when they could retire on half-pay. Or they could complete thirty years and receive two thirds pay. Robbie would have to wait. Whilst he was waiting he got on with the job and he loved it.

CHAPTER TWENTY EIGHT

Now here was the detective inspector outside this shop where a hysterical woman was being comforted by a man who stood on the pavement with his arms wrapped around her. He stopped long enough to get the general drift of what was going on. He didn't dilly or dally or faff about. This was a time for decisions and Robbie was good at making decisions and making them fast. He went straight through the door into the shop like a torpedo into the side of a ship. He knew there was a man in there with a gun. That didn't stop him. He found Cass still sitting on the floor holding the Luger. He saw the sergeant's stripes and the wine-red medal ribbon on Cass's chest and knew immediately who this man was. All Australia had waited for their VC to come home and here he was at the scene of a crime with a pistol in his hand. Gently he put his arm round the soldier's shoulders, lifted him from the floor and said, "Come on, mate. Let's go." Cass said not a word. Robbie took him to the door of the shop where he handed him to a uniform sergeant.

"Take Sergeant Carrington and the lady back to the station. Hold them in separate rooms. Don't ask them any questions until I return. If there are any witnesses get their particulars." Then he dashed back into the shop. An ambulance officer came rushing into the shop just as he knelt down beside Eric Dickson. The medic looked at the pool of blood on the floor, grabbed for Dickson's wrist, felt for and found a faltering pulse and said, "This man's in a bad way. We have to move fast."

Dickson was placed in the ambulance. Robbie McKye jumped in behind the medic. The ambulance took off hell for leather with its lights flashing and siren wailing. It was an exercise in futility. Dickson wasn't going to make it. The medic tried his best to stem the flow of blood. Dickson was conscious but was gasping for breath. The medic looked at Burns and shook his head. Burns knew what he must do. He took out his official police notebook and began to write furiously. He took from Dickson a Dying Declaration. It began as is recommended in the police training-school manual how all such documents should.

'I Eric Dickson, make this declaration
believing that I am in hopeless and certain
expectation of imminent death…'
It ended with the words,
'then we both had our hands on the gun.
I don't know what happened. I felt a terrible punch
in my stomach. I had been sh…'

Whatever Dickson was going to say he took to the grave with him. As far as Cass was concerned he had said too much. The medic and the DI both signed the statement which became part of the evidence in the case of R v Carrington.

Robbie went back to his police station and there interviewed Kitty. He knew that he must obtain a statement from her as a matter of utmost urgency and priority. Any good police officer knows that they must strike while the iron is hot. While the wound is red raw and throbbing. Take the statement from the witness immediately after the incident occurs and they are likely to get the unvarnished truth. Give the witness time to think and what they are likely to receive is what they witness wants them to receive not what actually happened. Kitty told it exactly as it happened. A statement was then taken from both removalists.

The one who had put his arms around Kitty and attempted to console her repeated word for word what she had said. They were words he was never likely to forget. They were very powerful words not likely to be very helpful to Cass in a criminal trial for murder.

The shop had been sealed off and a police officer stationed outside. The premises were subjected to a microscopic examination. Everything that could be photographed was photographed. The bundle of letters was seized. The kit-bag was seized. The Luger was finger-printed. Goodness knows why - wasn't he found holding the gun? Kitty and Cass were finger-printed. DI McKye went to the morgue with the fingerprint officer. Dickson's body was taken from the fridge and his prints taken. No stone was left unturned for Robbie knew that this case would have ramifications the like of which Australia had never previously experienced.

When he thought he had the full story McKye had Cass brought from the cells where he was being held to an interview room. There with a detective sergeant to take notes. He first cautioned him telling him that he didn't have to answer any questions but that anything he said would be taken down in writing and might be used in evidence. And there McKye's investigations hit a brick wall. It was a wall the nature of which he had never met before. Cass just sat there staring straight ahead and never uttered a single word. He had not uttered a single word from the moment Robbie had led him from the shop. Robbie was gentle in his questioning. He knew that the softly softly approach was ever to be preferred to the big stick. He knew too that he was dealing with a VC holder and that this man was not going to scare easily or be in the least intimidated by anything he would say to him.

95

"I just want to hear your side of it, Sergeant Carrington. I have no axe to grind. I think I know where you are coming from. All I want to know is what happened. Was the gun yours? Did it go off by accident? Was it the deceased who pressed trigger? I give you my word of honour that I do not wish to charge you for murder if it can possibly be avoided. Please don't tie my hands. Give me something to hang my hat on. Something that will get you out of this scrape."

It was useless. Cass just stared straight ahead. Not once did he speak.

For the first time in his life Robbie McKye was stumped. He took the matter to his Commissioner who passed the buck to the Public Prosecutor's office. It was there that Richard Fullilove got his teeth into it. That little man with his hunched back, piercing blue eyes and the point of his nose so blue it competed with his eyes for attention. That nose was not blue from drink. The Public Prosecutor didn't drink or smoke. That was just the way his nose was. And he was not married either and never would be.

CHAPTER TWENTY NINE

It was said that Richard Fullilove had a mind like a clam. Anything that went into it was never allowed to escape without his say so. He had instant recall and he lived for the law. He hated criminals. To him they were a festering sore on the face of society and the best thing for them was that they got their just desserts in full measure. No matter what their station in life; who they were or what they were they all had equal treatment from him. It was said that if his mother had farted in church he would have had her indicted for discharging a noxious substance in a sacred place.

He took the file, studied it very carefully then went to see the attorney-general. It wasn't for guidance that he went to see the A-G; he was too conscious of the independence of his office for that. It was simply to alert him to what he was about to do. The A-G was a political animal well skilled in passing the buck. He hared off to the premier immediately like a greyhound after a rabbit and brought him up to date with what was happening. The premier was a wily old bird who knew his Public Prosecutor. He had experience of his intransigence in the past. Looking the A-G directly in the face he said, "What will be will be. Justice must take its course." And that was that."

Two days after he had stepped through the door of Eric Dickson's shop Cass was formally arrested and charged with murder.

The media went into paroxysms of rapture. They had a story beyond all stories. A Victoria Cross holder caught up in the middle of a love triangle alleged to have committed murder. This would sell newspapers. The banner headlines said it all: IT IS ALLEGED VC WINNER CAME HOME TO KILL.

CHAPTER THIRTY

"I arrived by boat in Melbourne just after Cass was committed for trial before a judge and jury. The family brought me up to date with what had happened so far."

Clarence Fitzgerald's pleas for some kind of acknowledgement from Cass that he understood what was going on were of no avail. Cass just stood to attention and stared straight ahead.

Richard Fullilove sat watching every move while the magistrate attempted valiantly and patiently to obtain some kind of response from this defendant. When His Honour failed the prosecutor rose to his feet, all one hundred and sixty centimetres of him and said, "May it please Your Honour, I would respectfully submit that this court be adjourned so that the defendant can be examined to determine whether he is mute of malice or mute by visitation of God."

There was a deathly hush in the court whilst His Honour looked directly at this little man.

After a long pause the magistrate spoke quietly in reply, "No, Mr Fullilove I don't think we should follow that course. At the moment Mr Carrington is appearing unrepresented. Before we move further in this matter my view is that counsel should be briefed so that his rights are fully protected. I shall adjourn until 10am tomorrow to allow that purpose to be achieved."

"As Your Honour pleases," intoned the Public Prosecutor.

The following morning as the hands of the court clock touched ten the magistrate stepped through the door of his chamber to the bench. The court orderly called "SILENCE IN

COURT. ALL RISE." The magistrate bowed and sat. The public sat too. The crowded court was in session.

Julius Lawless was on his feet. "Don't you think Lawless is a good name for a lawyer, Ben?" Grandpa chuckled.

I replied that I thought it amusing but hardly more so than the prosecutor's. "I think, Grandpa, that anyone on the receiving end of a brutally incisive cross-examination from a person with that name would not think the prosecutor was full of love."

"You don't know how right you are, Ben. I can tell you Richard Fullilove was a tiger unleashed when it came to his cross-examination of a witness."

"May it please Your Honour," said Julius lawless, "My firm would like to represent Mr Carrington on a pro bonus basis but I am having difficulty in receiving instructions from him. He just isn't communicating. It isn't that he has refused our services; he just isn't saying anything. May I have Your Honour's permission to represent him nevertheless?"

"You may indeed, Mr Lawless. If your firm had not undertaken his defence I should have had to appoint one from the public purse. The court is grateful for your interest. Now, do you need more time to examine the evidence or are you in a position to proceed?"

"I understand, sir, from my learned friend, Mr Fullilove, that the court has had the same difficulty in communicating with my client as I have had and the question has arisen as to how best to proceed. As far as I am concerned at this point, sir, I am at something of a loss. So far as a Preliminary Inquiry is concerned I am quite prepared to forego that procedure and have my client committed to the higher court for trial before a judge and jury of his peers. By so doing the defendant and the witnesses will be excused the trauma of having to go through what is almost tantamount to two trials. Then the question of his ability to plead may be determined by the higher court. If necessary, sir, he could in the interim be examined as to his mental state. As he is not required to plead at this juncture I will have opportunity to examine the evidence, may even be able to communicate with him and in any event be in a better position to conduct his defence."

A ghost of a smile flitted across Mr Fitzgerald's face. Julius Lawless was no slouch. His submission if accepted deprived the prosecution of the chance to traumatise the witnesses at a PI and leave them shaking when they went into the witness-box a second time at the trial proper. There wasn't much the prosecution could do about that either. The whole purpose of a PI is to establish that there is sufficient evidence to go before a jury upon which they could, not necessarily would, make a finding of guilt. It was a neat move in the circumstances. Mr Fullilove had no option but to consent. So he consented. Cass was remanded in custody for trial before the higher court.

It was March 1946. Cass was before the court again. A higher court this time. He stood in the dock surrounded by a sea of wigs and gowns. His Honour, Mr Justice Pinkersun, sat in the seat of high control looking down at all those around him. His Honour just had to blink to send a shudder down the spine of the person careless enough to cause that blink. This was an environment that was even better controlled than a highly trained army drill squad for here no one shouted. The pieces fell into place almost by magic. The judge's clerk sat in front of him; the only person in court allowed to sit with his back to the judge. Cass in the dock sat facing the judge immediately behind the bar table at which sat counsel for the prosecution and the defence and their assistants. The jury sat on the judge's left. The witness-box was on his right.

The representatives of the media had their own allocated seating area and it was packed. Those of the media who couldn't find a seat there sat at the forefront of the court with their shorthand notebooks at the ready. They were not going to miss a word if they could help it. Various court officers were scattered about: the court orderly who called the witnesses, the jury keeper, the officer who attended to the exhibits, the officer who escorted witnesses to the witness box, the officer who opened and closed the door. The trial proper was about to begin.

There had already been a trial of sorts. A jury had been empanelled for the sole purpose of establishing why Cass wasn't talking. That submission of Richard Fullilove's that Cass be examined to establish if he was mute of malice or mute by visitation of God had been taken up. Eminent psychiatrists and psychologists had examined him whilst he was on remand in prison. During all of their examinations not one of them got a word out of him. He just sat and stared straight ahead as if they weren't there. Those learned personages came up with a variety of diagnoses that cost a fortune but didn't do much for justice one way or the other. At the end of their smoke and mirrors and bamboozlement the matter was put to a jury. The jury wasn't paid a huge fortune but in my opinion had a lot more common sense than all those quacks put together. When asked how they found after their one hour's deliberation in the jury room the foremen rose and said that their unanimous finding was that Mr Carrington, and he said Mr Carrington, was a perfectly normal person who was doing what he was entitled to do and that was to hold his tongue and if the prosecution had a case to prove it should get on with it and stop wasting time. This man was in custody and the sooner the trial was over and done with the better justice would be served.

"I can tell you, Grandson, that finding, and the way it was delivered, sent a rocket up the rear-end of the powers-that-be and gave an inkling of how the man in the street felt about the case. No way were they going to find that a man who had put his life on the line for his country had any malice for anyone or wasn't loved by his God. I can tell you, Ben, that on that day more than ever I was proud to be an Aussie."

~ THE ENDING ~

CHAPTER THIRTY ONE

"The trial began on a blistering hot day and I was the first person ushered into the witness-box. I can tell you, Grandson, I didn't want to be there."

As soon as I had arrived home and been brought up-to-date by my Mum and Dad and Elsie with all that was happening I went to the prison to see Cass. I told the prison people who I was and they seemed very glad to see me. "Maybe he'll talk to you," said the prison officer who interviewed me. "He certainly won't talk to us and all we want to do is to get him to talk so that we can all hear his side of it. We all want to hear his side."

It was a forlorn hope on the part of the prisoner officer. When he was told that I had arrived at the prison and wanted to speak to him they got not the least response from Cass. It was as if he had never heard of me. As if we weren't best mates and hadn't slogged across Europe and fought side by side together for endless months. Those prison people were good people; they did their best. In the end the prison warder did what he shouldn't have done and took me into the depths of the prison to Cass's cell door. There he dropped the hatch and allowed me to look into the cell. I looked through and there saw Cass sitting on the bare boards of his bed his eyes wide open staring straight ahead.

"To say I was shocked by what I saw is to put it mildly. This was not the Cass I knew. His hair had gone white and he only in his mid-twenties. White, I tell you, Grandson. None of those clued-up psychiatrists and psychologists who had examined him could explain that. They didn't have to. When Asked by Julius Lawless what they made of it everyone of them, and they were all men, in their smart suits, collars and ties and their soft fingers, said that was something to which they had not applied their minds. Their function had been to establish why he was standing mute; it was not to comment on his physical appearance. And he was so pale and thin. Even thinner than he was the first day I met him at the army training camp. He had become a different person."

For a flicker of a moment I thought the prison officer had got the wrong cell. I sucked in my breath and was about to speak but the prison officer was ahead of me. He spoke in a whisper. "Yes, he has changed, I'm sorry to say. He is not the same man as he was when I first saw him. It's such a terrible shame."

My heart hit my boots. I thought, 'What the hell have they done to him?' I wanted to kill somebody for what had been done to my old mate. But who was I to kill? Who was I to blame? A thousand thoughts went through my mind. What could make a man so vibrant, so full of life, into a white-haired zombie overnight? My old mate was suffering the torments of the damned. He was in his own private hell. How could I help him?

The stark truth was that I couldn't help him; nobody could help him. Well, maybe one person could but she wasn't there to tell him she loved him and so he suffered.

I said, "It's me, Cass, Rad your old mate. How you going?"

No reply. Just that unblinking stare.

I tried another tack. I knew that he loved Kitty. Would never stop loving her. So I said, "Kitty's okay. Mum and Elsie took her from the hospital to our place when the hospital said she was fit to be discharged. You know she had a terrible shock after what happened in the shop and was in hospital for three days. Mum visited her there every day. When the media found out where she was they were round the house like a howling pack of hyenas round a fresh kill. There were people with cameras surrounding the house, photographing every move. Even looking in the windows. The police seemed unable to control them. I wanted to turn the garden hose on them but the police said if I did it would be common assault and even that wouldn't stop them. They were in a feeding frenzy. Nothing could abate them. In the end Elsie took Kitty to her place late one night. She's there now. Still the media are camped out around our house, the bastards. Mum doesn't mind as long as it gives Kitty some relief. So you don't have to worry about her. I'll look after her. We'll all look after her. So please talk to me, Cass."

It was no good. He just wasn't responding. I tried and tried and tried until at last the prison warder whispered, very gently, "I'm sorry, mate. He's not going to answer. Nobody and nothing will make him answer. I think he just wants to die."

He closed the hatch and as we walked side by side back to the admin office he said, "Poor bugger, I feel so sorry for him. If I had been in his shoes I'd have done the same. I'd have put a bullet in that mongrel who was shagging his wife." He gave a wry laugh then and said, "Prison officers are not supposed to talk like that. Putting a bullet in someone is against the law. You didn't hear that."

"I can tell you, Grandson, that prison officer rattled me. There he was as good as saying that he thought Cass was guilty. If he thought like that what would other people like him, ordinary people, sitting on the jury, think?"

The prison governor, himself, was waiting at the admin office. That surprised me. It showed me just how human those people were. They all seemed to be on Cass's side. Looking at me with his eyebrows raised and a quizzical look in his face he asked, "Any luck? Did he speak to you?"

I couldn't speak. I just shook my head.

"What a pity. I was hoping you could help."

CHAPTER THIRTY TWO

"That was one of the worst days of my life. As soon as I got out of the prison I went round the corner, sat down with my back against a wall, put my head in my hands and blubbered. Yes, Grandson, your old grandpa blubbered like he had never blubbered before, not even when he was a kid. The rest of that day is still very much a blank to me. When I got home I went straight upstairs, locked myself in my room, threw myself on the bed, buried my face in the quilt and howled. I stayed there until the next morning. All the time I wondered what I could do for Cass. At that time if I could have taken the rap for him I would have as long as it would have meant he could be with his Kitty. I think I might still have been in that room if my mother hadn't called me to say there was a police officer there who wanted to speak to me."

A police officer to speak to me. I thought. What could he want? Surely they don't think I have done anything wrong in going to see Cass. Surely they don't think I am in some way implicated in all this. I got off the bed, straightened my rumpled clothing and went down to see him. D.I. McKye was sitting on a bar stool in the kitchen with a cup of tea in his hand talking to my mother. As soon as I entered the kitchen he put down the cup, slid off the stool, came towards me and stretched out his hand. I was relieved, I had done nothing wrong.

Addressing me by my first name he said, "I'm Robbie McKye, Rad. The detective inspector in charge of this case, Rad. It's been a tough call."

He told me that the prison people had told him I had called

and what had happened and he wondered if I could assist him.

"I don't think you can help Cass directly," he said, "but maybe you can help him indirectly by putting me better in the picture."

"Help you?" I said. "You have pinned a murder-rap on my mate. Do you want me to sell him down the river as well? Do you want me to ram your case home?"

"No, Rad. Not at all. That's what I don't want. What I want to know is what really happened in that shop and why. As for pinning a murder-rap on him, well, look at the evidence. It doesn't leave me much option. I'm the one who found him in that shop with a gun in his hand, a man dying on the floor in front of him and his wife outside screaming that he had said he would kill that man and had killed him. What was I to do? What I want from you is anything that will let me get into his mind. He sure as hell isn't letting anyone in there at the moment. He's not even saying it was self-defence, which might help me to help him. There is a defence of provocation but I don't think that would fit here. Maybe if I could say that he was so traumatised by his wife's behaviour with another man that he didn't know what he was doing, it might help but that is a long shot and I would need professional medical and mental people to help me with that. The truth, Rad, is I'm scrabbling in the dark."

"I have no intention of saying anything that will damage my mate. He probably saved my life a dozen times. No, I'm saying nothing till I have thought this thing through."

"I know where you're coming from, Rad, but it's like this. If you don't give me something voluntarily the Public Prosecutor will subpoena you. And I can tell you this, mate, when he gets you in that witness-box before the judge and jury he'll put the frighteners on you in a way you can't imagine and he'll chew you up for ass-paper." His voice hardened a little. "The choice is yours, mate. You can do it the easy way or the hard way. If you do it my way it might just help your mate. I'm not promising, mind you, but it might be better than your way."

My mother spoke then and said, "I think you should listen to what the officer is saying, Rad. It seems like good advice to me."

I ignored my mother. I was on to this police officer with his 'I need your help. Help me out in this.' Oh, sure, fill in the gaps for me. 'Help me to send your mate to the gallows.' Nobody was going to put the frighteners on me. Who did he think I was, some callow youth who didn't know what day of the week it was? I had been places where this smart-arse cop had never been and never would be. I was not that slow. In those days a conviction for murder meant hanging. Even as Robbie McKye spoke I visualised the Mr Justice Pinkersun sitting on his high and mighty throne in court donning the black cap over his wig and intoning in a pseudo-mournful voice, 'Cassidy Ambrose Carrington you have been found guilty of murder by a jury of your peers and it is my sorrowful duty to sentence you to be hanged by the neck until your body be dead. And may God have mercy on your soul.' The thought chilled me to the bone. I saw the hangman pull the lever and Cass with his hands pinioned and a black bag over his head fall through the trapdoor kicking and fighting for his life. No, I was not going to assist any cop to do that to my mate.

If Cass wasn't talking neither was I. So I told the detective inspector to go to blazes. If he wanted some kind of stool pigeon he had the wrong man. And the sooner he left our house the better I would be pleased. I was so mad that I lost it completely. I told him if he didn't leave our house now, that minute, I'd throw him out.

My mother put her hand to her mouth in horror. Robbie

McKye didn't turn a hair. He put his hands up palms outwards and said simply, "It's okay, Rad. I know you're trying to be a good mate and I appreciate your position but I really am on the level. I'm not out to put a rope around the neck of a man like Cass Carrington. I'm just sorry that I find myself in the position of the axeman. But that goes with the territory. If you change your mind you know where to find me." He left with his dignity more intact than mine.

CHAPTER THIRTY THREE

Many times since I have regretted how I spoke to Robbie McKye then. He was only doing what he was paid to do, but then again, I was only being loyal to a good mate.

My mother was furious with me. "What's wrong with you, Rad? Can't you see the officer is on our side," she said. "I believe he genuinely wants to help Cass. Now you will be subpoenaed. Just you wait and see."

"Yes, Mum," I replied, "and a little pink pig just went flying past our window."

I wasn't subpoenaed. Richard Fullilove was too far ahead of the game for that. He knew what he was doing. I didn't. Oh, yes, he knew very well what he was doing and how to do it. He arrived at our house two days later just after dark. My father answered the knock on the door. He identified himself and asked if he could talk to me alone. My father invited him in, showed him into our lounge-room and offered him a seat there. He didn't sit down and was still standing when I joined him there. My father withdrew and shut the door quietly.

We stood facing each other. I hadn't seen him previously. Only heard of him. He had taken off his soft hat on entering the house, as was the custom on those days. He was dressed in a pin-striped suit with waistcoat, a white shirt with stiff collar and a tie. The tie was probably his old school or university tie. About a centimetre of the cuffs of his shirt peeped out from the end of each sleeve and the same measure of a whiter than white handkerchief showed itself from the breast-pocket of his jacket. A gold watch was in his left-hand waistcoat pocket. Its chain, with fob, was strung across to the pocket on the opposite side.

"There were few wrist watches in those days, Ben, and the time-pieces were all winder-uppers. Battery-powered watches were something the future would bring, much to the chagrin of those little gnomes in Zurich."

His black shoes had a shine many a guardsman would have envied. And his hair had a parting so straight I thought he must have used a spirit-level to make it so and there wasn't a hair out of place. Even taking off his hat hadn't ruffled it.

I took all this in at a glance and knew that I was standing in the presence of a perfectionist. That perfection didn't do anything for me except to make my hackles rise. If he was this meticulous about his personal appearance what must he be like in court? Robbie McKye's warning that he would chew me up for ass-paper came back to me.

My hackles rose even more when he identified himself to me. His voice reminded me of cold clear crystal water running down a mountain stream. Every word was enunciated so softly clearly and distinctly. I have often heard it said that some people with words alone could charm the birds off the trees. Richard Fullilove was a barrister; he belonged to the fraternity of wordsmiths. It was by the spoken word that this little man standing before me made his living. This was the man who was prosecuting my mate. This was the man who would try to convince a jury that Cass was guilty of murder and should be hanged. I will confess that my hatred of him at that moment was unreasonable. I hadn't heard what he had to say yet. My first impulse in my hatred of him and my loyalty to Cass was to take him by the scruff of the neck and the seat of his pants and throw him through the door, open or closed, into the street. These people don't give up, I thought, now they are harassing me. They are trying to intimidate, sweet-talk, cajole, coax or coerce me into doing something completely alien to me. He must have felt the vibes because he raised his hands and said. "No, Mr Bruce, I haven't come here to harass you or in any way coerce you to do something against your will or conscience. What I have done is to come here to put you fully in the picture. You see there are some things of which I am convinced you have no knowledge. Listen to me for a moment. You don't have to speak. If when I am finished you want me to leave I will do so. Is that clear?"

He had piqued my curiosity. I said, "Well, I suppose that's fair. We might as well sit down. I don't mean to be ill-mannered but loyalty looms large in my scheme of things."

He sat and said. "Thank you." He was extremely polite throughout.

Folding his hands in front of him he said, "Let me pose a question which I will answer myself. How well do you know your friend? Your answer to that will be, better than anyone else, maybe better than his wife, Kitty. All right, I'll take that to be your answer. Now, my next question, which I will not answer but I hope you will is, do you know that he is a deserter?"

You can imagine the effect that question had on me. It was as if I had had a hard slap across the face. It sent my senses reeling. What was he talking about? For a moment I couldn't think straight. My mind went blank. I knew that if I could see myself in a mirror my mouth would be hanging open. The only word I could utter was an explosive, "What!"

"I thought so. I'll repeat the question so that there is no doubt you understand what I am asking: Did you know that your mate is a deserter?"

"It's a stitch-up!" I said. "I've been with Cass for years. He's no deserter. Deserters run away from war. Cass ran into it. He was always at the front leading us. He's the bravest man I've ever had the good fortune to call my mate. He saved the lives of me and our other mates a dozen times. You're making it up. What's going on?"

"I can assure you, sir, I am not making it up. I don't make things up. That's not what I do. Your mate is a deserter. You'd better hear the full story. I assure you I can prove everything I am about to tell you. You won't know either that his name isn't Cassidy Ambrose Carrington?"

I shook my head in disbelief. I didn't know. There was something not right here. I was in the middle of a bad dream. My visitor continued.

"His name is Charles Anthony Clark. You see, the same initials. Very handy when your life is a sham. If you are initialling documents you can't go wrong when you are using the same initials you have grown up with. In a forgetful or distracted moment you can't get it wrong. And he isn't from Narrogin in Western Australia although he may have visited there on his peregrinations around Australia."

"Your mate was born to a single mother in Katherine in the top end of Australia. She loved him and cared for him until he was fourteen years old. At the tender age of thirty two she was struck down with ovarian cancer and young Charles was left to fend for himself. His mother hadn't made many friends. She was ashamed of her fall from grace for at that time to have a child out of wedlock was a great disgrace and she did not want this son she loved so much to be shamed by her sin. What was the boy to do? Well, it seems that he roamed around this big land of ours getting such jobs as kept body and soul together until the outbreak of war. He was then of the age to join the Royal Australian Navy. There he found family and all went well during training. It was only when his training was finished and he went to sea in a small ship that his troubles began. Why is not within my knowledge but it appears that he may have had some inner ear trouble that caused him to be violently sick when the sea became rough and the vessel gave a wobble. Poor fellow, it seems that he struggled valiantly to keep going and do his job but in the end it all became too much. He couldn't eat or drink because if he did it all went over the ship's side."

"What was he to do? He applied to the captain of the vessel to be transferred to the army for he felt that as a fighting man in the navy he was more of a hindrance than a help to the war effort. The captain was an old salt, very well-intentioned but with no idea of the young man's plight. He pooh-poohed the idea of a transfer saying: 'This is the senior service, sailor. To go into the army is to go down a peg. We can't have that. Did you know that Admiral Lord Nelson was sea-sick every day and look at the record he left. I have no doubt that you will get over this in time when you get your sea legs. It's just a matter of hanging in there. Application dismissed.'"

"He was so wrong. The young sailor knew he would never get his sea-legs. He became thinner and thinner and whiter and whiter and had he remained at sea would, I am sure, most certainly have died. Young Charles did the only thing he could. When the vessel docked at Sydney he gave two fingers to his captain and did what I hope I would have the fortitude to do in such a situation, he jumped ship. No, he didn't run from the war. Running from the enemy was not for him. He went directly into the city, bought himself a pair of shorts, a singlet and thongs and went round to the army recruiting centre and joined the army. The army didn't ask too many questions. There was a war on. They needed fighting men and here was a young man volunteering. Within a week he was at the army camp where, I suspect, sir, you met him. Do you think I might have got it right thus far?"

While he was talking the wheels in my brain were flying furiously. Now it all became clear. The drill sergeant picking up that he had drilled before. That salute of his. That was a naval salute with the fingers to the middle of the right eyebrow and the palm inwards. It was the way the old sailors working with tarry ropes hid their dirty palms when saluting an officer. And no luggage, only a razor and a toothbrush when we first met in our billet. Now I knew why he threw himself into soldiering like his life depended on it; like he had something to prove. He had: that he was no coward. Gawd, I am slow, I thought. Why hadn't I picked this all up before?

Reluctantly I said, "You might."

"I don't think I need to say any more about that," he said. "What I want you to know is that this knowledge stays with you and me. Only my immediate staff know about this. Also, his former naval officer, who saw his picture in the paper, recognized him and got in touch with me. I have sworn him to secrecy. None of my staff will speak out of turn on this because if they do they will be former public servants and they will never get another job with us and they sure as hell won't get a reference. No, sir, I am not covering up. Covering up is something I don't do. What I have just told you has no bearing whatsoever on the charge with which Mr Carrington stands before the court. It is too remote. Has no proximity. Publicising it would have no value except that the media would have a field day. I mention it only to inform you that I do not consider it my function to kick a good man, any man for that matter, when he is down. What I want from you is what you can tell me about your mate's relationship with his wife, how they met and how the marriage was. I want you to go into the witness-box and tell the jury the kind of man you know as Cass Carrington to be. You can write your own statement and I will examine you on oath on it. I will not pull any punches but I will not play any dirty tricks either. All I want are the facts. You see, Mr Bruce, I prosecute, I do not persecute. Are you with me?"

"What could I say, Grandson? This little Quasimodo, for that was how I unkindly thought of him before I met him, had won me over. I admit that I had hated him, quite unreasonably. In my unreasoning I had not heard the other side. I said he would have my statement the next morning."

"Thank you, Mr Bruce. I pray that what you say will help justice to be done," he said as he rose from the chair. The interview was over.

I asked him if he would like a cup of tea. He declined saying, "I have much to do and must be on my way. Thank you for your hospitality."

I walked him to the door. He bowed to me, replaced his hat and was gone. The next time I saw him was across the well of the court as I stood in the witness-box.

CHAPTER THIRTY FOUR

I sat up late that night pondering what to do. I looked at the matter from all angles. In the quiet of the night it came to me what I must do. Cass must be protected no matter what. In my mind I knew that the prosecution had those letters and would have read how Cass said he would kill Dickson as soon as he set foot on Australian soil. I would tell the whole truth and at the same time paint Cass in the best possible light. The next morning I took my statement to Richard Fullilove. He read it through in my presence, smiled and said, "Thank you Mr Bruce, I'll see you in court."

It pains me to say it but I was the first witness for the prosecution in the case against my friend. But it wasn't all bad. Things went along much as I thought they would. Each question I was asked I answered apparently without having to think about them. That I thought would impress the jury. The prosecutor's examination-in-chief was nearly over. I was over my initial nervousness and was congratulating myself on how I had dodged any curly questions, not that there were many curly questions. Richard Fullilove simply asked me to tell the court in my own words how well Cass and I knew each other. I went through it all from the day of our first meeting in our billet until the day I stood in the witness-box. I told how he met his wife, how they were married, how happy they were together and how he hated the separation.

"When you were overseas how often did he write to his wife?"

"He wrote every day except on those occasions when it was

impossible to do so."

"And how often did he receive letters from his wife?"

"Every time we had mail he had mail. Sometimes he had several letters together."

"Did you see any of those letters?"

"Yes."

"Did you read them?"

"No. They were his letters not mine."

"Did he share with you the contents of those letters in oral form."

"I didn't want to know what was in the letters. They were between him and his wife."

"Wasn't he upset on one occasion and didn't he show you one of those letters?"

"Yes."

"Will you please tell the court about that?"

"There was a lull in the fighting. The mail came. Cass received several letters. He took them and went off to read them in private as he usually did. When he came back I saw he was white and trembling. When I asked him what was the matter he didn't speak. Instead, he just handed me a letter and insisted that I read it. I did so reluctantly. The contents shocked me. It was from his wife, Kitty, telling him that she had been unfaithful. I commiserated with him. I truly felt for him for Kitty was his life."

"What happened then?"

This was the question I had prepared for. "Cass was very upset."

"How do you know?"

"He was white and trembling."

"Did he make any comment?"

"Yes. He said what many of us soldiers said when somebody

or something had upset us. He said he would kill the mongrel; he would cut his balls off. But I knew he didn't mean it. That was just his way of getting rid of his anger. We all talked like that. If one of our mates did something objectionable such as blowing smoke in our face, or spitting or sneezing without putting a hanky to their face somebody was likely to say, 'Do that again, you dirty so and so and I'll knock your brains out,' or, 'I'll kill you.' Soldiers often said, 'I'll murder the little bugger,' when they were referring to some peccadillo committed by a mate. Cass Carrington was a very well adjusted man. Sure he went out each day to kill the enemy but that was in defence of his country. To murder a fellow Aussie, that was not him."

"I have no further questions, Your Honour." Richard Fullilove sat down.

"Julius made no objection and left well enough alone. He was very wise. Richard Fullilove had allowed me to express an opinion without interrupting me. Opinion is as you know only too well as a lawyer, Grandson, something only experts are allowed to express in our criminal courts."

"I was not cross-examined and was relieved to step out of the witness-box. My ordeal was over. I hadn't known before that the witness-box is a torture chamber. You will no doubt remember that, Ben, when you are pinning some poor unfortunate fly to the wall of the witness-box. Now I was able to sit in court and see the whole drama unfold before me."

CHAPTER THIRTY FIVE

The second person into the witness-box was Stan Roberts, removalist. He took the oath and the prosecutor took him through his evidence, which was very basic. "Me and my mate, George, were carrying a sofa into a house up the street when I heard the screams. I looked in their direction and saw a young woman standing on the pavement. George and I dropped the sofa and ran to her assistance." He then began to repeat what he had heard Kitty say.

Julius was on his feet in an instant.

"I submit, Your Honour, that what this witness wishes to testify to cannot be admitted in court for several reasons. First it is hearsay. For the benefit of the jury hearsay is something a witness has heard another person, not the defendant, say out of the presence and hearing of the defendant. The defendant at that time was not present. Not only is it hearsay but as that wife cannot be compelled to testify against her husband such words allegedly spoken by her cannot be admitted in evidence by some indirect route. I submit that any reference to such alleged utterances be stricken from the record."

Julius sat down. Richard Fullilove rose.

Quietly, without the least hint of rancour in that melodious voice of his, he said, "Your Honour, I agree entirely with what my friend has said about hearsay and a spouse's non-compellability."

I could see some of the jurors straining forward as the prosecutor spoke. Was some important and deadly part of the evidence to be omitted?

That was not going to happen. Not with this prosecutor. He was a prosecutor and he was, as his sartorial elegance proclaimed, a perfectionist.

He continued. "I submit, Your Honour, that what this witness is going to testify to is neither hearsay nor evidence against this defendant which his spouse could not be compelled to give. It comes under the provisions of res gestae rule, i.e. things done in the story of what happened from beginning to end. It is an inextricable part of the evidence and it forms part of a well-travelled route to justice in the history of jurisprudence."

There was no answer to that. His Honour agreed with him and Stan Roberts was allowed to tell the story as he knew it to be. Stan Roberts was a decent man. I'm sure it caused him as much pain as it caused me for him to relate truthfully and totally what he knew had happened that day to the detriment of a man who had earned the VC fighting for his country. But he had sworn to tell the truth the whole truth and nothing but the truth and he was stuck with it.

He repeated word for word to the court all that Kitty said and all that he saw until a police officer removed Kitty from his arms and took her and him to the police station.

"How good is your hearing?" asked the prosecutor.

"My hearing is very good. I've never had any trouble with it."

Almost under his breath Richard Fullilove asked, "What time is it?"

I could see some members of the jury straining forward for they hadn't quite caught what the prosecutor had asked.

Stan Roberts didn't miss a beat. He looked at the court clock and said, "It's ten minutes past eleven, sir."

He had stopped Julius from claiming that his hearing was defective. Richard Fullilove didn't miss much.

Julius asked no questions. To do so would have been to hammer home what Stan Roberts had just sworn to.

The testimony of George Kelly the next witness corroborated what his mate had said and then we were on to Robbie McKye.

CHAPTER THIRTY SIX

Detective inspector Robert Burns McKye stepped into the witness-box, raised the bible in his left hand and took the oath. Yes, it was his left hand. Contrary to what most people believe the bible does not have to be taken in the right hand. Either hand will do. Robbie was left-handed and so naturally took the bible in that hand. That astute little martinet, Fullilove, watched every move as Robbie handed the bible back to the court orderly and sat down. He didn't have to watch this witness so intently for he had taken Robbie through his evidence in several previous cases. But that was his natural wont and so Robbie was scrutinised.

Robbie was a good witness. He told the court the way it was. It was a classic case of, I was, I saw, I did. Only the facts were given.

Speaking in a firm clear voice he said, "There had been an emergency call relating to a matter of extreme urgency. I rushed to the scene and found a very distressed young woman in the care of a removalist called Stan Roberts. They were on the pavement outside the shop of Mr Eric Dickson, the deceased in this matter. As a result of what Mr Roberts told me I went into the shop."

He told the court what he had found and what he had done. He produced the Luger pistol, the bundle of letters and the Dying Declaration to the court. There was no difficulty with the pistol and the bundle of letters which were admitted into evidence. There was great difficulty with the Dying Declaration. Julius Lawless knew that was a damning document. He was on his feet attempting to establish in the greatest detail how that document was obtained. He did not want it in at any price. How did the deceased know he was dying? What was the cause of death? Oh, yes, he had died alright but what was it that killed him? It could have been a heart attack? Wasn't he known to have an irregular heart-beat? He was not in the best of health. Hadn't the army rejected him on three separate occasions? Robbie replied that the deceased knew that he was dying because the medico had told him how grievously injured he was and that he had no hope of recovery and that he should prepare to meet his Maker. In the making of the Dying Declaration he had acted in accordance with police practice. "I believe, sir, that the ambulance officer will be called to testify and he will be able to advise on why he thought Mr Dickson was in extremis. I am not a medical person. I was guided by him throughout."

Julius fought tooth and nail to have it excluded but he should have saved his breath. Robbie had done everything according to the book and there was just nothing Julius could do about it. The document was admitted into evidence and it too marked for identity.

Then came the letters. Robbie produced the great bundle he had retrieved from the shop. Again Julius became really excited. He didn't want those letters in. He didn't want them read in court for those were Cass's letters to Kitty in which he had declared his intention to kill Dickson at the earliest opportunity. He submitted that they were privileged documents. Were communications between husband and wife during the course of the marriage. To admit them into evidence could be construed as the defendant's wife giving evidence against him. That was something, his instructions were, she did not want to do.

At that the prosecutor interposed to point out to the jury that Kitty was not the client of the defence counsel. He could not take instructions from her. It may be that she would become a witness and testify on her husband's behalf and defence counsel could then take her through the evidence. The prosecution had yet to decide if it wished to call her. She could then decide of her own volition whether or not she wanted to give evidence. But that would be her choice. She was not the property of the defence. There is no property in a witness.

But so far as the letters were concerned it was a lost cause for Julius, they were admitted into evidence.

When the prosecutor said, "No further questions, Your Honour", Julius rose and began his cross-examination. He took Robbie through everything he had done at the crime scene. He had him look at the photographs of the interior and explain them to the jury. Each of the jurors was given their own copy of those photos.

"What was the space like behind the counter? By that I mean was there room for two people to move around there with ease?" asked Julius.

"Behind the inside of the counter and the rear wall was a rather confined space, Your Honour. It seemed to me that if two people wished to pass each other there it would be a tight squeeze."

"Would a stepladder be required to reach items on the higher shelves?"

"Undoubtedly so, sir."

"What about the storeroom?"

"It was a small room but there was ample space to move about in?"

"Were there items on higher shelves for which again a stepladder would have been needed to retrieve them?"

"Yes."

"Did you notice anything unusual when you were examining the interior of the storeroom?"

"The one thing that struck me was the strong smell of perfume. I noticed that there was no perfume for sale in the shop."

"Did you find anything else that struck you as somehow unusual in that storeroom?"

"Yes, I found a pair of knickers under a carton there."

"What did you do about them?"

"I did nothing, sir. There had been no complaint of any kind made to me that would cause me to probe further into the presence of that garment there. My duties do not include the gratuitous embarrassment of people who come within the ambit of my investigations."

"Quite so," said Julius and he sat down.

There was no re-examination and Robbie left the witness box to take his place behind the prosecutor at the bar table.

The ambulance man was next. He took the oath and sat down.

He told of arriving at the scene and finding Robbie attending to the deceased. The amount of blood on the shop floor alarmed him. His examination of the deceased caused him to believe that there was little hope of saving him. The deceased was conveyed to the ambulance but expired on the way to the hospital, but not before D I McKye had taken a Dying Declaration from him. He was handed the Dying Declaration, nodded and said. "Yes, this is that statement. That is my signature on it." He pointed to his signature.

"How much experience have you?"

"I have been an ambulance officer for 26 years."

"Were you in any doubt that the deceased was going to die?"

"None. That's why I told him so. I would not have told him so if I had been in any doubt."

Julius cross-examined.

"How did you know he was dying?"

"It was obvious, sir. Nobody could lose that amount of blood and survive. I was amazed he lasted so long."

"What killed him?"

"Loss of blood."

"Could his death have been caused by a heart attack?"

"It could have but he had no such symptoms. What he had was a gunshot wound to the stomach. I could see clearly the powder burns around the wound."

A pathologist was the next to give evidence. He told of his qualifications and experience and how he had given expert evidence of opinion in courts of all kinds on numerous occasions over several years. Julius did not object to his being accepted as an expert witness. He told of examining the body of the deceased in the morgue and carrying out a post mortem there. He said the body was that of a well nourished male. There was evidence of cardiovascular irregularity over a long period but not such as would have caused his death. It was quite likely that with proper care he would have lived into old age. There was no difficulty determining the cause of death. A firearm had been pressed against his abdomen and fired. The muzzle of the weapon had left an impression on his stomach. Powder burns could be seen surrounding the wound. The bullet had travelled upward, had nicked the aorta sufficient to cause the blood to pump out not in a great gush but in what one might call gentle spurts. The missile had then travelled across the body and exited through the left shoulder. It was not a massive wound and though there would have been great shock would not have been fatal had surgery been available. Without surgery there was no hope. Cause of death was clearly loss of blood causing cardiac arrest.

Julius did not cross-examine.

A ballistics expert next told how he had examined the pistol. He said it was a perfectly normal weapon with no defects. It did not have a hair-trigger and would have taken a good deal of pressure to discharge. It was unlikely to go off by accident.

Again Julius thought it better to leave well enough alone. To have cross-examined this witness would have been to press home the case against his client.

CHAPTER THIRTY SEVEN

The prosecution case was closed. Now it was time for the jury to hear the other side. Julius called his first witness. Danny Simmons' name was called. He walked into the court and up to the witness-box with hardly the trace of a limp but he did not sit down. That would have meant that he had to get up and it was not easy for him to get up with that artificial limb and he had his dignity. He took the oath and identified himself all the time looking at the jury. He said that he had known Cass for several years during their armed service and that he was one of the bravest and finest men he had ever known. Cass had saved his life and he told how. Indeed he killed the enemy as we all did but always according to the rules of war.

When Julius asked him if Cass was a wanton killer, he said he didn't know what wanton meant. Julius explained the word to him. Danny shook his head.

"Far from it," he said. "Not once did he kill needlessly. On one occasion I was behind Cass who had leaped over a wall. There in front of him was a young German who looked no more than sixteen. The Germans were running out of men and were sending beardless boys to the front. That boy had a rifle in his hand pointing directly at Cass. Poor boy he was so petrified with fright he couldn't pull the trigger. Cass swept the gun aside and punched him in the chin with his fist. The boy collapsed in a heap and was later taken prisoner. Cass could easily have killed him. Such slaughter was not for him. Then looking directly at Cass and with the tears streaming down his face he said, "I love you, Cass. We all love you." Cass still sat, immobile. I saw that most of the women in the jury were weeping. I wept too, Grandson. Danny had done his best for his mate.

George Sanders name was called and he was led to the witness-box by a court volunteer. His guide dog, Towser, sat just outside the box with his nose on the step. Not once did he take his eyes off his master. I looked at Towser and wondered if he would have liked to take the oath too. He didn't seem happy at being separated from his master even though by only such a short distance. Sandy's evidence was much the same as Danny's but was delivered very differently. George had difficulty with the pronunciation and enunciation of some words and had to repeat them sometimes more than twice. What he had to say was that Cass was a good mate, straight and true. He didn't do dirty tricks. Cass had saved his life. It was a pity that Dickson was dead but then Dickson had done the unforgivable and had paid the price. He had no sympathy for him.

In the middle of George's evidence Towser suddenly raised his head and looked at the jury box. In a flash he was up on all four legs, quivering, with his tail straight out behind him. Caring not for the decorum of the court he began barking loudly and he had a good strong bark. Everything in the court stopped. George could be heard clearly saying, "What is it, boy? What's wrong?" He reached out his hand for the dog to come to him. Towser stopped barking, went to the outstretched hand and had his ears fondled. He had done his job.

Towser had been ahead of all those present. Maybe even of the one-armed man in the centre of the front row who was clutching at his chest with his right hand and hyperventilating. His face had become cyanosed. His Honour leaning forward said quietly and firmly, "Mr Clerk ring for an ambulance." To the people in the jury he said, "Give him room to breathe." Then,

"This court is adjourned." He swept into his chambers. The juror was lifted on to the floor in front of the jury box. The ambulance man, who was still sitting in court, came, knelt beside him, took his pulse and shook his head. It was a hearse that was required not an ambulance.

The court stayed adjourned until next morning when His Honour advised with sorrow that the juror had been declared dead and that he would not abort the trial, which would continue with eleven jurors.

CHAPTER THIRTY EIGHT

What caused the juror to have a heart attack I don't know. I have often wondered about that. Was it the sight of George in the witness-box with that terribly ruined face? Sir Archie Macindoe, the great plastic surgeon of wartime fame who had put back together again the faces of many RAF airmen, had worked on that face. Even he had difficulty with the nose which wasn't a nose anymore and the mouth which had become and still remained a hole without lips. Maybe that face brought back to that juror the day he lost his arm in that other war in defence of freedom. Whatever it was we shall never know. All I could think of was that my mate was in the dock fighting the greatest battle of his life for his life and not saying a single word in his own defence. I couldn't understand it. What the hell was wrong with Cass? Why didn't he speak? What was he up to?

When George finished his evidence Julius called for a short break. When the court was back in session I was surprised when the orderly called Mrs Katharine Carrington and Kitty was led to the witness-box. She stood there white-faced and trembling, a slight figure dressed in a white short-sleeved cotton blouse and an emerald green skirt which cut across her knees. A strand of her lovely dark brown hair had fallen across one cheek. She swept it back with a quick nervous flick. There was a little gold locket at her throat which I knew Cass had given to her.

"I can tell you, Grandson, I gulped and wondered what Julius was up to. Anything Kitty had to say was unlikely to help Cass. What could she possibly say that would help him? Her utterances outside the shop had gone a long way towards putting the rope around his neck. How could she retrieve it? I prayed that Julius knew what he was doing."

I looked at Richard Fullilove. He was sitting erect behind the bar table. Maybe he too was wondering what Julius was up to. We were both to find out before the hands of the court clock reached the hour where an adjournment was called for. Of one thing I was certain, before she stepped out of that witness-box she and the husband she said she still loved would be stripped naked before a body of strangers eager to immerse themselves in the intricate workings of a marriage between a brave man charged with the murder of the man who had stolen his wife's affections and the wife who wanted both men. I watched as she took the bible in her hand and read in a quavering voice the oath from the card the orderly held in front of her. Then she sat down.

Julius gave her a moment to compose herself. Not too long for that would surely have made her more unsettled than she already was.

"Tell the court who you are."

"I am Katharine Carrington. The defendant is my husband."

I looked at Cass. He sat unblinking and immobile, still staring straight at the coat of arms behind the judge's head. It was as if he was in another world. Maybe he was.

"Will you please tell the court why you have come here?"

"It is because I want my husband to know that I still love him. Always have. Always will."

"You are aware that you don't have to give evidence? A wife cannot be compelled to give evidence against her husband."

"Yes, you have made that clear to me."

"You know that the prosecutor, Mr Fullilove, may ask you questions in cross-examination that you will have to answer?"

"I know that and I don't care what he asks me. I just want

my husband and everyone else to know what really happened. I know I have sinned and it's all my fault that my husband is here. I betrayed him but I don't think I'm as bad as I have been made to appear in this court."

"Would you please tell the court how you met your husband and what led to his being charged with the most serious offence on the criminal calendar?"

Kitty, sitting slightly bent forward with both hands between her knees and looking at a spot just above the jury-box, told of her first meeting with Cass.

"Elsie Bruce is a very good friend of mine. It was her wedding reception and I was seated beside this man I had never met before. I was very nervous. I am a very solitary person and hardly knew any of the people there. I kept my head down and pretended to concentrate on the speeches and the food but I wasn't really enjoying it. I was afraid to look up and was wondering how I could make an early exit when in a lull between one of the speeches the man beside me turned to me and whispered in a gravelly Humphrey Bogart-like voice, "What is a good-looking dame like you doing in a run-down joint like this? Why aren't you in Hollywood among all the other models?"

"For a moment I wondered if he was addressing me. It couldn't be me. No man had ever spoken to me like that before. Then I plucked up courage and turned and looked into his face and my heart leapt. He was smiling at me, the most entrancing smile I had ever seen. At that moment I knew that this was the man for me. The thrills ran up and down my spine. I don't know how I managed it but I was able to stutter, 'I only came here because I knew you would be here.' He laughed such a throaty, hearty laugh. And from there we didn't stop talking for the remainder of the night. Our conversation was so free and easy it was as if I had known him all my life. I don't know what was said in the speeches but I remember every word he said that night. He told me afterwards that for him it was love at first sight, that he had never met anyone like me. It was as if we had been destined to meet at that wedding reception. I told him that I felt the same. He was a soldier on leave from the army to attend his friend Rad's sister's wedding. We spent every day of the remainder of his leave in each other's company."

"That was a time when I experienced a bliss I had never known before. I didn't think it would last. I thought that I was just a plaything that he'd forget when he got back among his mates. I am glad to say I was wrong. A day after he arrived back at his unit I had a letter from him. I couldn't believe my good luck. I had a letter from him every day after that until the day we were married. I have all those letters still."

"I remember our wedding night, the first night of our honeymoon. At last we were alone; far from the madding crowd. We were in our hotel bedroom. I was extremely nervous for I didn't know what to expect. I confess that I had fantasised about that night and what would happen. Now it was upon me. I was quivering because I was about to enter the unknown. I had never seen a man naked before and no person, man or woman, had ever seen me without clothes. Indeed, I hardly dared look at myself naked. I didn't think it was the thing a young woman should do."

"He took me in his arms and kissed me and I kissed him back. He said, 'I suppose you will want to get ready for bed?' I said. 'Yes.' I slipped out of his arms and went into the bathroom and changed into my PJs. When I came back into the bedroom he was already in the bed with the sheets drawn back for me. I slid in beside him. He covered me with the sheets, took me in his arms hugged and kissed me. I shall never forget that night. I was carried aloft in his arms up into the stratosphere to land on cloud number seven; the cloud nearest heaven. And every night for our all too short honeymoon it was the same. Short though it was we got to know more about each other than some other people do in a lifetime. Up to the moment I met my husband I was a sleep-walker. I slumbered my way through life having not the least idea what life was all about. He taught me that life was meant to be enjoyed. That we were on this earth to enjoy every minute of our being. That our destiny was in our own hands and if we didn't enjoy it then we were dead-beats who didn't deserve the life we were given."

"'You have to get out there, Kitty, and grab it with both hands for you never know the minute it might all come crashing down. Don't ask any questions. Just go for it,' he said."

CHAPTER THIRTY NINE

"When the honeymoon was over and he went back to his unit I was very lonely. I missed him so much. I went back to work and tried to pick up the pieces but it was no good. I missed those nights in his strong arms. I wondered if this was what being a soldier's wife was like - she only achieving bliss in small doses. What was I to do? After that honeymoon there was no other life for me. I wanted to be with my husband and had decided that I would drop everything and travel up to where he was and be with him, regardless. Surely I could find somewhere to live. Surely we could work something out. But I didn't have to. One glorious glorious day a telegram arrived telling me to come immediately if not sooner; my husband was waiting for me. I was on the next bus and we were back together again. And what a togetherness that was. Our honeymoon was like an entree before the main course. Those seventy two days that we spent together in old Mrs Rafferty's house were the closest I shall ever be to heaven in this life. Apart from our honeymoon they were the full extent of our married life together. The house had such a good feeling about it that I felt blessed from the moment Cass picked me up in his arms and carried me across the threshold. His good friend Rad Bruce melted into the background."

"He had permission from his commanding officer to spend his evenings and sometimes weekends at home with me. I waited every day for four o'clock when I would hear his knock on the door and ask, 'Who is it?' Sometimes he would answer 'It's the big bad wolf I'm coming to get you.' The door would open, I would shout, Oh, no, no, no, and run. He would chase me all over the house. I would leap over small tables, ottomans, around large tables and chairs and any obstacle in my path until I was breathless. When it was coming up to the time of his arrival I would take Raskal to the bathroom, put him in there and close the door. I did that because when Cass was chasing me around the house Raskal would run too, barking and yelping, enjoying the fun as much as we did. On one occasion I tripped over him and went head over heels on to the couch. It was a great game. The chase always ended in the bedroom where Cass would take me in his arms, hug and kiss into ecstasy and make love to me. Afterwards we would end up in the shower together. He said that showering together was the best way to save water which was a scarce commodity. I would wash his back and he would wash mine. We were madly in love and I was the happiest wife in the world. Happier than I had ever been in my life."

"At other times when he knocked on the door and I asked who it was he would say, 'It's the doctor. I have come to give you your happiness injection.' I would reply that I had an injection yesterday and the day before that and the day before that. He would laugh and answer that I needed it every day; it was what made my cheeks bloom and my eyes sparkle, that he had his syringe all loaded up and ready. At other times he would say that he was the doctor coming to take my temperature and that he had his thermometer ready to insert. Always I replied that I trusted him for he was the best doctor I ever had; that his surgical procedures always worked and that it was magical how they could cure me of all my aches and never leave a scar. He was not like the doctor who took out my appendix and left a scar that I still have. His reply to that was that it was a reciprocal thing because I could cure him of the rheumatism from which he had suffered since he was a teenager. A little time in bed with me and all his stiffness was gone. It was all rather silly, wild, maybe even reckless but we didn't care. We both knew that he might be called away at any minute and we had to make the most of our lives while we could. He was my husband and I loved him as I had never loved before and I knew he loved me just as much."

"I shall never forget the day he arrived at the door along with Rad Bruce. He asked who I was and then said that he had brought a friend to guard and protect me when he wasn't around. On that day he handed me a kelpie-cross pup which I called Raskal. That was the Raskal who was to get under my feet when he chased me. That was the best present I ever had from any person. He became my best friend next to Cass. When Cass wasn't there he always slept beside my bed at night. The first thing in the morning when I woke up I would pat his head and he would lick my hand."

"Cass and I tried to forget the war and act as if it had nothing to do with us. And, really, it was so far away. But it had a lot to do with us. We were living in a fool's paradise. The whole world was at war and we were part of the world. One terrible day the war made its presence felt. My husband, my beautiful, dear kind caring loving husband was gone far away and I was left alone with only Raskal to comfort me."

"The night before he left we didn't sleep a wink. We made love all that night. I tried to be brave and not cry but I couldn't help it. The thought of his not being there broke my heart. He told me to be strong, that as soon as the Germans heard he was coming they would surrender en masse. It didn't help. I still wept. The days that followed were the loneliest I ever experienced. The worst part was I didn't know where he was. Then his letters began to arrive and I didn't feel so bad. His letters were always censored and it made me angry that someone else was reading our private correspondence. But that was war and I had to accept it. I wrote to him every day. He would tell me how he dreamed of me and dreamt he was operating on me. I told him that I wished it wasn't a dream that what I wanted was the real deal. I wanted him home to operate on me every day. I can tell you it was hell. It was hell because I was alone and I didn't know if I would ever see him again. And what would I do then?"

"Being in the house alone without him was too much. I cried myself to sleep every night. Sometimes there would be a gap between his letters and I lived in agony expecting every day to receive a letter telling me I was a widow. Then several letters would arrive together and I would breathe again. Other wives surely went through the same as I did but they had people around them to give them some measure of comfort. I had no one. I went down in the dumps. The dumps became even worse when I lost Raskal. He ran into the road after a ball and a car hit him. After that I couldn't live in that big empty house anymore. It had lost its spirit and become cold and dreary. I packed my bags and returned to Melbourne to live with Rad's parents. After a while I found a place of my own to live in. I was too miserable to live with anyone else and I didn't want to be an old misery-guts. I got my own place and got a job in Ricky Dickson's shop. That was a great help but it was the worst thing I could have done. It was fine to begin with. I had purpose in my life again but things took a turn that I never could have imagined or foreseen."

"Ricky and I were often alone in the shop and I would tell him how I missed Cass. He would comfort me and tell me not to worry, that the war would end soon and then all would be well. Sometimes in the storeroom when I missed Cass very much I would sit down on a crate, put my head in my hands and cry. Ricky would catch me weeping sometimes and tell me things would be alright."

"It was a very hot summer and that may have contributed to what happened next. It was a very confined space behind the counter and when Ricky and I were there we often had to touch each other as we squeezed passed. I would often put my hand on him or he would put his hand on me as we did so. I thought nothing of it. Being so close I felt the need to shower two, sometimes three times a day. I used perfume regularly. I shed as much clothing as I could. On most hot days I wore only a blouse and skirt. I didn't wear anything underneath. It may be that at that time I gave Ricky the impression I was coming on to him. I never did. If I did it was an unconscious thing."

"One day in the storeroom I was particularly low. I hadn't heard from Cass for several days and wondered if maybe he had been killed. If maybe I was a widow and didn't know it. How terrible that would be. Things just got on top of me again and I dissolved into tears. That was when Ricky came in. On that day he did what he had never done before. He put his arms around my shoulders, lifted me up, pulled me close to him, hugged me and said it would be alright, he would look after me. The next thing I knew he was kissing me on the lips and, worse still, I was kissing him back. I just couldn't help myself. Almost before I knew what was happening I was against the wall and he was making love to me."

"It was only when it was over that I realized the enormity of the terrible thing I had done to my dear husband. I had committed adultery and betrayed the person I loved most in all the world. I was so shamed of myself that I ran home and didn't leave the house for three days. I didn't eat during that time. I just lay in bed and wallowed in my guilt."

"In the afternoon of the third day I heard knocking at the

door. I pulled myself from the bed and went to answer it. Ricky was there. He was very apologetic. He said he didn't know what came over him; it was just that at times he felt as lonely and alone as I felt. He came into the house. I started to cry again. He put his arms around me and hugged me again. And I was kissing him again. I don't know why. I was very mixed up. I needed someone there to comfort me physically. We ended up in bed. The next day I went back to work. Ricky and I made love in the storeroom. It was all downhill from there. Every day we made love. I moved in with him. All the time I was wracked with guilt. What had I done to Cass? Surely he would never forgive me. Then in some stupid way I thought if I wrote and told him what had happened and how, he would forgive me, and Ricky, for you see it wasn't all Ricky's fault. I was afraid too that if I didn't tell him he would hear it from someone else and I wanted him to hear my side of it first. I thought that maybe when he came home we could talk it over like civilised human beings, Ricky would drop out of the picture and all would be hunky dory again."

His reply didn't help. He said he forgave me, that Ricky had taken advantage of me when I was at a low ebb, that he could not forgive him and I was to leave his employment immediately or there would be dire consequences. Now I was in a quandary. I really didn't know what to do. Ricky was being very good to me. I needed his loving. I could not go back to that empty house to be on my own, staring at the four walls all day. And so I replied to Cass that I couldn't give Ricky up; that I was sure we could work something out. Cass's replies left me in no doubt at how unhappy he was. Now I really was lost."

"You see, I didn't know if Cass would ever come back to me. He was doing such brave and reckless things that I thought one day his luck would run out, I would receive that dreaded telegram and then what would I do? The thought of being alone again with no one to love me petrified me. In some way I don't understand even now how I had come to depend on Ricky more than I realized and while maybe I didn't love him as much as I loved Cass I loved him a little. And so I dithered. Every day I had prayed for the war to end. Now my prayers were answered and I didn't want them answered. The war was over and Cass would be home very soon. I hadn't expected him to arrive back so quickly but one day out of the blue the shop door-bell rang and there he was at the counter facing Ricky with a pistol in his hand. What happened then has become a blur. There was a terrible argument between my two men. Ricky was dragged over the counter and they were wrestling on the floor. I heard a bang and I don't know what happened after that. I came to myself in hospital. It was then that I learned Ricky was dead and Cass charged with his murder."

"I want only to say this. My husband is not a murderer. He is the most gentle, kind, loving person I have ever met and no matter what I shall always love him. I beg for his forgiveness. What happened was my fault as much as Ricky's. Maybe even more mine than Ricky's. I ask you, the jury, to set him free. Acquit him of this crime he did not commit. Please send him back to me so that I can make amends for all the suffering I have caused him. That is all I have to say."

CHAPTER FORTY

"I had wondered, Grandson, why Kitty was recounting all these very intimate and very personal details. They didn't seem to me to have a lot to do with the offence with which Cass was charged. Now it all began to make sense. Remember, it was 1946. At that time females, even Aussie females forthright though they are, did not strip themselves naked in front of a courtroom full of strangers. Didn't tell what went on in the bedroom or out of it. What Kitty was doing was showing how terrible was her betrayal of the first man to ever love her with a love that was so all encompassing. She had let him down. She was the sinner not him. It was all her fault. The court, especially the jury, had to learn how human he was, how fragile. She must have thought that there were people in that jury just like Cass and her who would understand, who would forgive her her adultery and set her Cass free."

There was silence in the court for a few seconds before it became clear that she had finished her long narrative. Richard Fullilove sat for a few seconds with his head down looking at his papers. It passed through my mind that he was not going to cross-examine. Then he stood up. He was, after all, the prosecutor. His job, what he was paid to do, was to put before the court the facts as he had them and that he must do.

He was very quiet, very gentle. "Mrs Carrington," he said, "there are some questions I must ask you. This has been, is, a harrowing experience for you but the court must be advised of the facts before it can reach a verdict, whatever that verdict may be. I regret that that being the case there are some questions which I must ask. I will make your trauma as brief as I can."

"Did your husband ever threaten to kill Ricky Dickson?"

There was a long pause while the court waited in breathless suspense for the further act of betrayal.

An almost inaudible, "Yes."

"Did he declare that more than once?"

"Yes."

"You see, Grandson, Kitty could say no other for all those threats were in the letters found in Cass's kit-bag outside the shop. If she had not agreed then she would have shown herself to be a liar and all of her plea to the jury would have been brought to naught. The witness-box truly is a torture chamber."

"How did he do so?"

"In his letters to me when I begged him to forgive Ricky."

"Look at these letters."

The orderly handed her some letters. Kitty looked at them.

"Are those the letters?"

"Yes."

"I ask, Your Honour, that these letters be admitted in evidence."

Julius made no objection to the prosecutor's request. He knew it would have been futile to do so.

"Now tell me, Mrs Carrington, did your husband hand Ricky Dickson a pistol and tell him to kill himself?"

"I can't be sure. It's all a blur."

"Did you run into the street saying that your husband had killed Ricky Dickson, that he said he would and that he had done it?"

"I don't recall that at all."

"Look at this document."

Kitty took the document the orderly handed to her.

"Is that your signature on that document?"

"Yes, it looks like it."

"Did you make that document?"

"I don't know. I can't remember."

"But you can't deny it's yours?"

"No."

The document was admitted in evidence.

"Thank you, Your Honour. No more questions."

Julius re-examined.

"How well do you know your husband Mrs Carrington?"

"Very well, I think."

"Do you think when he made those threats to kill Ricky Dickson that he meant them?"

"That is evidence of opinion which this witness is not qualified to give," objected the prosecutor.

"I submit that this witness is an expert on her husband. She knows him better than anyone else," countered Julius.

"That's a novel submission, Mr Lawless but I regret it doesn't hold water. Objection sustained," said His Honour.

There were no more questions. Kitty's ordeal was over.

CHAPTER FORTY ONE

The defence closed its case. Both counsel summed up for the jury.

Julius kept his summation short. Cass Carrington had suffered a grievous betrayal. He had one love in his life. That love had been taken at a low ebb in her loneliness and she had done the unforgivable. Ricky Dickson was the author of his own misfortune. Cass Carrington had never meant to kill him. What the defendant had done was attempt to throw a scare into his rival for his wife's affections. He had handed him the pistol and told him to kill himself knowing full well that that request would not be complied with. In his anger he had pulled the deceased over the counter and there was a struggle for the weapon. Undoubtedly that pistol had killed Dickson but who had pulled the trigger? Cass Carrington was found with the gun in his hand. That didn't mean he had pulled the trigger. Who pulled that trigger or how the weapon was discharged was a mystery that the court would never solve. Cass Carrington had killed lots of men. He had done so in defence of his country and liberty. He did not do so wantonly as Danny Simmons had pointed out. That young German boy who had pointed a weapon at him and who had been knocked senseless to save his life could have testified to that. Certainly the defendant killed other innocent men. That is what men do in war. That was what he had been trained to do. That does not mean that he killed a fellow Australian. The bible says Thou Shalt Not Kill. Yet people do kill when the reasons are justified. The bible says Thou Shalt Not Commit Adultery but people in their humanness do commit adultery. But there is never any justification for adultery. The difference so far as this court is concerned is that there is no punishment for adultery on this side of the Great Divide. The punishment for murder is to die fighting for life at the end of a rope. Therefore, ladies and gentlemen of the jury, before you commit Cass Carrington, VC to that end, when he will pee his pants and empty his bowels, you better be sure that you have got it right beyond a reasonable doubt because thou shalt not err. If you have a doubt, a reasonable doubt, and ignore it, you will live with it for the remainder of your lives. I believe you to be decent men and woman who will do what justice is screaming out for in this case. That is that you acquit the defendant and send him back to the woman he loves."

Richard Fullilove stood up, pulled his gown up over his misshapen shoulders and in that clear, crystal, musical voice of his put the prosecution side. What he said was short and to the point. He laid only the relevant facts before the jury.

"Ladies and gentlemen this is probably the saddest case I have ever had to prosecute. Before you stands one of the bravest of men. He didn't just get one medal for bravery, he got three. Does that permit him to kill what the defence counsel described as wantonly? A superfluous question. Of course it doesn't. In the eyes of the law all men, be they prince or pauper, hero or coward, are equal. There is no discount for being a hero."

"I ask you when considering your verdict to look only at the facts. You must do that as you have sworn to do. That is your duty. You have heard all the witnesses. You have heard the defendant's wife's impassioned plea. What do the facts show? That's what you must ask yourselves. I contend that they show indisputably that the defendant was advised by his wife that she had betrayed him. He took it badly. He wrote not once but on several occasions that if the relationship did not end he would kill her lover. The relationship did not end. He arrived back in Melbourne and did what he said he would do as soon as his feet touched Australian soil. He dodged the welcoming committee that awaited him at the airport, went straight to the shop where Ricky Dickson was, behind the counter. He was armed with the pistol he had had in his possession for some months. No doubt he had formed the intention then to kill his rival. He presented that pistol to Mr Dickson and asked him to do the right thing. That was to commit suicide and thereby redeem himself from the sin of adultery. When Dickson refused he was dragged over the counter. There was a terrible struggle at the end of which Mr Dickson lay dying. Before he died the deceased made a Dying Declaration. Signed and witnessed by the detective inspector and the ambulance officer. That statement said it all. I regret to say, ladies and gentleman that the facts show a clear case of premeditated murder. You have no choice but to find the defendant guilty of murder. Thou shalt do your duty."

Richard Fullilove sat down. His Honour addressed the jury.

He gave them a short resume of what both the prosecutor and defence counsel had said, to refresh their memories, I suppose. Then he told them how he saw it and how they might wish to look at the evidence. They were to consider the facts and only the facts. They were not to be swayed one way or the other by what they might have heard outside the courtroom or by the defendant's position in life. They were not lawyers. They were ordinary citizens whose purpose as a jury was to determine beyond a reasonable doubt whether the defendant was guilty or not guilty. I noticed that he did not tell them what a reasonable doubt was. His summing up was very fair. It was clear to me that he was remaining completely neutral, leaving it to the jury to

154

decide Cass's fate. When he had finished he put them in the care of the jury-keeper and sent them out to ponder the evidence.

CHAPTER FORTY TWO

"Now, Grandson, as you know, what happens in the jury-room is sacrosanct. Only the jury knows what happens in there. That is the way it is and the way it should be. However, it so happens that I know some of what went on in that jury-room. I won't tell you how I know but I do know. I know what Jim Baker and the foreperson said. All else was a babble of voices with no identification as to who was speaking."

"I know that big Jim Baker was first into the jury-room and he was seething. He stormed into the middle of the room, turned round and faced the other members as they entered."

"That bloody prosecutor," he said. "He wants us to hang Cass Carrington. Well he won't be hanging him as far as I am concerned. A man who goes out and places his life and limb in danger every hour of every day and wins the VC and two other medals for gallantry while the prosecutor, the judge and all those other bozos in there were sitting safe and snug can be sure that I am not going to assist their judicial murder. They frig about with their fancy words and their Res Gesty, or whatever the hell it is, and expect us to do their dirty work for them. They mouth the words and tell us we are the judges of fact and it is for us to decide the prisoner's fate. We are the ones to do the hanging. The blame is going to be on our heads. Well, it won't be on me. I don't know what the hell was going on in there. I'm a roofer, I'm not a lawyer. I wouldn't know a fact from a fart. I've never been in a court in my life before but what I know is this, I'm not for hanging a man who did what I would have done to any man who was shagging my wife while I was out there keeping them safe. If you ask me Mr Friggin' Dickson got what was coming to him. If it had been me I would have handed him a grenade with the pin out just to let him know that I didn't love him. His days of shagging another man's wife while that man was out fighting for his country would have been over. I'm voting for an acquittal. The rest of you can do whatever the hell you like."

Jim stood there hyperventilating, glaring at those around him.

The well-padded lady who became the foreperson said, "Now, now, sir. That's not how we are supposed to go about deciding our verdict. We are supposed to consider the facts carefully, calmly and deliberately, without emotion, prejudice or bias, come to a unanimous decision and then advise His Honour what that decision is. But, sir, before we do anything else we must first select a foreperson to act as a kind of chairperson and put our views on this matter through that person. Now I would like to pose the question, who wishes to nominate for foreperson?"

There was a deathly hush in the room. There wasn't a volunteer to be seen. The lady wasn't in the least put out. Most people were looking at their feet. The lady spoke again. Addressing Jim she said, "I would propose that you, sir, take on that role. You can lead us in the debate to decide if we should let a murderer go free or let the world know that we have charged an innocent war hero with the most serious crime of all. What do you say to that?"

"I say that I'm not foreperson material. I have never been in charge of anything in my life and I'm a bit too old to start now. I don't want to be here. I would rather be up on a roof from where I can watch the rest of the world go by. What I think is that you are the best person for that role. I nominate you."

"And I second that," said a male voice from the other nine.

"I think, Missus, that you would make a good foreperson.

You seem to know what this is all about."

There were several murmurs of assent to that proposal and as there were no other nominations and the lady who was called Elspeth didn't object she was 'volunteered' into that exalted position by a unanimous decision of her fellow-jurors. That was the only unanimity to follow in that jury-room for the remainder of the time its occupants were incarcerated there. Then began in earnest the battle for Cass Carrington's life.

"I can tell you, Grandson, there was little cool, calm, emotionless and deliberate consideration of their verdict by that jury. At times so heated was their debate that their voices rose to fever-pitch and the jury-keeper began to wonder if murder would be done in that jury-room. She could hear some of the hubbub through the solid core door outside of which she stood guard."

Sometimes everybody wanted to speak at once. Sometimes there was a single voice calling for calm and careful reasoning. They got neither.

"We're here to consider the facts."

"The fact is that sod Dickson got what he asked for."

"That's not a fact."

"What the hell is it then? He's dead, isn't he? That's a fact. That's why we're here."

"We have to determine who pulled the trigger."

"How the bloody hell are we going to determine that?"

"Well Cass was found with the gun in his hand. Doesn't that tell you who pulled the trigger."

"It tells you nothing of the kind. He could have picked the gun up afterwards. If he was cunning he could have left the gun beside the body."

"Yeah. But he didn't do that and his fingerprints were on the trigger."

"Of course his fingerprints were on the trigger. Wouldn't his fingers automatically go there when he was holding the gun?"

"He brought the gun to the shop."

"Yeah. To throw a scare into Dickson. If he had wanted he could have waited until Dickson was alone in the shop and killed him then. Instead, he fronted him while his wife was there as a witness. People don't deliberately commit premeditated murder in front of witnesses."

"Oh, don't they? Are you an authority on when people commit premeditated murder?"

"He killed Ricky Dickson and he intended to kill him. So VC or no VC we have to do our duty. After all we took an oath to that effect."

"The simple fact is that a man is dead because he was shagging a hero's wife. Are we now to hang the hero when we don't really know who pulled that trigger? I can tell you this. I'm with the big fellow. I'm for the roofer. He's knows more about justice than all those other bozos with their wigs and gowns in there put together. I'm for acquittal."

"You might be for acquittal, mate. I'm for doing what I swore to do and that is to do justice. Just because a man is a VC doesn't mean he is above the law and can murder anyone he likes. I'm for finding guilty."

"It's all the fault of that little tart of a wife. If she had kept her knickers on it would never have happened. Other wives had to wait for their husbands to come home. Why couldn't she?"

"I don't suppose you have ever been lonely in your life. Put yourself in her place. She didn't know if her husband was ever coming home and she had nobody there except Dickson to give her comfort."

"Yeah. He gave her comfort alright and plenty of it. I think he was more about giving himself comfort. He sure as hell was into giving comfort to soldier's wives. I think he was more into the wives or at least one of them. I'm for acquittal. Guys like Dickson are a festering sore on the face of humanity. Carrington should have had been awarded another medal for calling him out."

"To me it's all crystal clear. Carrington's wife told him that Dickson was keeping her happy. Carrington decided there and then to kill Dickson. Why else would he bring that gun home? Why else would he tell Dickson to shoot himself and if he didn't he would? Dickson ended up with a bullet in the belly. What does that tell you? It tells me that Carrington set out to murder him. He couldn't wait to get at him. He dodged the Governor's reception at the airport in his hurry to kill his wife's lover. It's as clear as the nose on your face. Carrington is a murderer. I don't care what you lot think I'm for abiding by my oath. I'm for finding him guilty. If you others haven't the guts to do your duty well, at least I have. I'll sleep content tonight."

And so the battle raged around big Jim Baker. Apart from his initial engagement with the foreperson he just sat there and allowed the others to get one with it. Occasionally the foreperson would call a halt and ask for a show of hands on a proposal for or against a guilty or not guilty verdict. And always big Jim's hand went up for not guilty. The other nine could have saved their breath. It was quite evident that big Jim was not going to change his mind. There was never going to be a unanimous verdict. Big Jim wasn't alone; three of the six women were with him. Elspeth and the two other women were for hanging. The remaining four men were two for two against. At length Elspeth gave up in disgust saying that there was no justice in that jury-room. It made her ashamed to be an Australian.

Shame or not she was never going to get those other ten jurors all of the same mind. She was a Don Quixote jousting at windmills.

To give her her due, she attempted to do what she had sworn to do and to do it without emotion in assessing the evidence. She must have been the only one in that room without emotion. She stood before His Honour and told him there was no agreement and was never likely to be any. Anyone attempting to read her face would not have learned from it the battle royal that had taken place in the jury-room.

CHAPTER FORTY THREE

I agonised for the several hours the jury were absent. It was the worst period of my life. Danny Simmons and George Sanders agonised with me. We kept praying for an acquittal. Every minute seemed like a fortnight. Danny said that the longer the jury was out the better. That meant that they were having problems agreeing. That was a good sign. When the jury came back to ask the judge what would happen if they couldn't decide either way that gave us all hope. We were clutching at straws. We dug our nails into our palms. We couldn't sit or stand still because of our nervousness. I would rather face a regiment of Jerries than go through all that again.

His Honour told the jury that they must do their best to bring in a unanimous verdict. If they couldn't do that it would mean that there would have to be another trial and nobody wanted to put the defendant or the witnesses through that again. The jury went back out to ponder again. The battle in the jury room raged into the middle of the night. At last the jury came back and said they just could not agree. There was no hope of a unanimous verdict. His Honour spoke to them and begged them to go out and try again. It was useless. They went out but came back in less than an hour and said they could not agree; that there was no hope of an agreement. His Honour had no alternative but to act on that decision or rather lack of a decision. He thanked the jury, though to do so must have made him grind his teeth, terminated the proceedings and adjourned court for a retrial date to be set. I heaved a sigh of relief. Cass was safe for the moment. He was led down to the cells by the prison officers. I went to see him. He still wouldn't talk to me. Just sat in his cell staring at the wall as if I wasn't there.

"You know what happened after that, Grandson. There was another trial when all the witnesses were put on the rack again. This time all twelve jurors, thankfully none of them died, couldn't reach a unanimous decision. Obviously, there is more than one big Jim Baker in Australia. After their foreperson, who was a man, told the judge of their inability to come to a decision one way or the other the prosecutor stood up and advised His Honour that there would be no further trial. In accordance with tradition there having been two trials in both of which the jury could not reach a determination the Crown would not proceed further. Cass was off the hook.

Those Aussie juries were not so slow. They were not going to make a finding of guilty or not guilty. They knew when to leave well enough alone. They didn't condemn Cass; they didn't exonerate him. They knew what they were doing. Any man who takes advantage of a little lonely girl whose husband was out there fighting and doing terrible things to keep Oz safe should know that nobody would worry too much if they got what was coming to them.

His Honour advised Cass that his ordeal was over and he was free to go back to his wife again. That statement told me that the judge knew people. He certainly knew Cass. Looking at His Honour it did not appear to me that the inability of those two juries to reach a unanimous verdict worried him in the least. He seemed relieved. Richard Fullilove shook hands with Julius Lawless. He didn't seem to have any hard feelings. He had done what it was his duty to do. The two prisoner officers patted Cass on the back and whispered something to him which I could not hear. They led him back down to the cells where I dashed to meet him. He still didn't speak a word. I said, "Come on, Cass, you are coming home with me." He didn't reply.

We went to the admin office, collected his things and waited a little while till the hubbub had died down. The police were very good. When it was dark they slipped us both out the back way to the underground car park. We both got into the back seat of a police car and lay down. The police drove out past the waiting media hounds. In the street at the rear of my parents' house they dropped us off. We went through the back gate and in the back door to the sitting-room where Mum and Dad were waiting. The three of us threw our arms around Cass and hugged and kissed him and wept. He wept too and spoke for the first time for months.

CHAPTER FORTY FOUR

"Thank God that's over. I'm sorry, Rad, that I didn't speak to you before but this was something I had to do on my own. I had got myself into this jam and I was going to get myself out of it or perish. One thing I was not going to do was to involve you in any way if I could avoid it. Neither was I going to speak in my defence or in any way say anything for or against myself. My fate was going to be decided by twelve Aussies who would hear all the evidence and either hang me or acquit me. I didn't care if they found me guilty. One thing I wasn't going to do was to plead. You and I, Rad, had faced death many times. It held no terrors for me. It's a pity that they didn't acquit me but I won't hold that against them. Somehow I knew they wouldn't find me guilty. Where was any prosecutor going to find twelve Aussies without at least one person who wouldn't be on my side? I couldn't see any hope of a unanimous verdict. I'm free and I won't argue about that. Now I can get on with my life. Where is Kitty? I want to talk to her."

My mother told him that Kitty was staying with Elsie and that he could see her that night. My father went and fetched Kitty. I shall never forget that meeting. She came into our lounge-room where Cass was standing trembling. As soon as she came through the door she threw herself into his wide-open arms. He wrapped them around her and pulled her to him. They were both sobbing. Mum, Dad, Elsie, Bob and I were also sobbing. We cleared the room. We left them to it. I don't know what they talked about but later that night Bob drove them to his and Elsie's house. He told them that it was their house for the night.

That he and Elsie would stay with Mum and Dad for the time being. They could ring when they wanted to see us.

That's almost the end of the story. It was a week later when they rang us and we all went to see them. They couldn't come to our house because the news vultures were still circling and even we had a job dodging them. When we eventually arrived at Elsie's place I was amazed to see the change in Cass. I hardly recognized him. He had dyed his hair back to dark brown again and had a week's growth of beard. He was almost back to his old self. The news hounds would have difficulty recognizing him. Kitty had dyed her hair blonde. It suited her. They said they were moving on. They would not tell us where they were going but they were moving to a place where they could be left alone and have that privacy that they both needed more than anything else. They thanked us for all that we had done for them. Cass put his arms around me and said if he was a Buddhist and I was better looking he would surely have married me. That was his parting joke. I drove them to the train station and there Cass left Kitty for a few moments while he spoke to me in private.

"Now, Grandson, that you have heard the full story what do you think of justice? That justice that you are going to spend the remainder of your life serving."

He reached his hand across the table and picked up the package that had been there throughout his story. He told me the package had been delivered a couple of days earlier. This was the last communication he had had from Cass. Every year since he last saw Cass at the train station he had a birthday card and a Christmas card from him. They always came from different locations. They never contained a return address. He opened the package and displayed the contents: a Victoria Cross, two medals for gallantry and several other campaign medals. There was a note from Cass. It said simply that by the time Grandpa received the package he would be gone to join his beloved Kitty who had died three months earlier. The big C had done for him what Jerry couldn't do. He said he wanted Grandpa to have the medals because he knew he would value them. They were as much grandpa's as they were his. No man ever had a better mate.

Grandpa said he was going to send those medals to Canberra where they could be put on display with all those other medals that Australia's sons have earned fighting and sometimes dying for what they believed.

"What do you think, Grandson? If you had been on that jury what would have been your decision?"

CHAPTER FORTY FIVE

I didn't know what to say. Grandpa had really put me on the spot. But then I thought, no, I won't dither, I'll make a decision. Dithering is not for me. So I said, "The evidence is so blurred that it is difficult to analyse with any degree of accuracy. I can understand the dilemmas of those two juries. If Cass had wanted to kill Ricky Dickson he could have done it another time when there were no witnesses about. The fact that he asked Dickson to kill himself indicates to me that he had no intention of killing him. I think that he was attempting to throw a scare into him or was giving him a little of the torture that Dickson had caused him over those months when Cass was pleading with Kitty to dump the mongrel. I would have voted for an acquittal."

Grandpa smiled and said gently, "You would have been wrong, Grandson, as I was. When Cass took me aside at the train station on the last occasion I saw him I said that I was sorry that he had been put through two trials for I knew all the time that he was innocent. Murder was not his style. He would never do something like that."

"He looked me directly in the face and said, 'You surely are a good mate, Rad. You always think the best of people, but you are wrong. I shot the mongrel deliberately. I said I would kill him and I kept my promise. I had killed many a young innocent German who was doing no more than fighting for his country like you and I, Rad. I have no regrets. God bless you.' He kissed me on the cheek, went to Kitty, took her hand and they were gone."

Printed in Australia
AUHW010451210819
316233AU00001B/2

9 780995 406889